PERISH PRIEST

RICHARD L. BALDWIN

To Thelma, my friend
Please enjoy
Rich Baldwin

Published by Buttonwood Press, LLC

P.O. Box 716, Haslett, Michigan 48840

www.buttonwoodpress.com

DISCLAIMER:

This story is fiction. While the real names of certain characters were used, the reader should not assume that words, attitudes, or actions are an accurate representation of the characters in this novel. This story has no purpose other than to entertain the reader.

ISBN 978-0-9972464-3-8
Printed in the USA

Cover photo credit:
Katarzyna Białasiewicz © 123RF.com

Published by Buttonwood Press, LLC
P.O. Box 716, Haslett, Michigan 48840
www.buttonwoodpress.com

Dedication

This book is dedicated to my mentor and friend, the late award-winning mystery author, **William X. Kienzle.**

Other Mysteries by Richard L. Baldwin

Acknowledgements

Thank you to my editor, **Anne Ordiway**; my proofreaders, **Joyce Wagner and Carol Johnson**; cover designer and typesetter, **Marie Kar** of Redframe Creative; and printer, **Bonnie Kahler** of Data Reproductions.

Chapter One

"Peace be with you," said Father Albert Dunkel.

"And with your spirit," the congregation responded.

"Let us pray." While most of the congregation stood with eyes closed, a muffled pop was heard. Father fell forward, hitting his head on the altar, and then fell back.

The congregation didn't know what to think. It happened so fast. Most thought Father had fainted for he hadn't seemed well for several weeks.

Dr. Dana Schafer, a cardiologist, immediately went to Father, pulled off his vestments and found a labored heartbeat. Father didn't respond to any questions. His collar was loosened and a seat from his chair helped prop up his head. The wound to the chest was obvious and first aid was administered.

Dr. Schafer got the attention of the lead usher, Don Adair, and told him to call 911. Most of the congregation walked outside, not wanting to interfere with the frenzied activity in the sanctuary.

The fact that Father had been shot had not registered with the congregation, and the doctor didn't want to create panic, so what the people didn't know was good.

Dr. Schafer was joined by a nurse and an usher who was told to keep people away. "Father needs air!"

Sirens could be heard in the distance as emergency vehicles drew near. One of the church leaders had gathered parishioners outside to pray that what they thought was a heart attack would be minor.

EMS workers rushed directly to the altar, where Doctor Schafer advised them of Father's wound and what vitals she could determine. "Pulse is very slow, he isn't responding to questions. I can detect a labored heartbeat. There's a gunshot wound in the chest area. We need to get him on life support and to the ER."

Father was given oxygen, and his chest wound was wrapped to decrease the chance of further bleeding. In the ambulance, the EMS team prepared Father for the trauma team waiting for them at the hospital.

As the gurney was wheeled out of the church, some people sobbed, some prayed, some shouted, "God bless you, Father."

Apart from the confusion in St. Joseph's sanctuary, the shooter was driving southeast on M-115, certain no one knew he had shot the priest. He was quite sure there were no security cameras in or about the church.

Mission accomplished was the thinking. Finally there was revenge and while Jesus made it clear that you must turn the other cheek and that an eye for an eye was not the way to grow spiritually, it didn't matter. The man losing his life, paid for the pain he had inflicted.

Despite efforts to save his life, Father Dunkel was DOA at the Mercy Hospital in Cadillac. The sheriff then informed the Bishop of Albert's death and that he suspected homicide. Fortunately, Father had received last rites.

Chapter Two

Mesick, Michigan
Twenty days before the murder

Mark Miller didn't like Father Dunkel. Actually he despised him and he didn't hesitate to tell others how he felt. Mark was 47 years old. He was slim with a receding hairline, and clean shaven. Since the day Father Dunkel celebrated his first Mass at St. Joseph's, Mark had built a mental wall and from that moment on, he wished Father Dunkel was out of St. Joseph's.

Mark's wife, Janet and daughter, Charlene, didn't share Mark's disdain. They didn't think he was the best priest they had ever known, but he was their priest and they accepted that reality.

Mark and Janet were among a group of founders of St. Joseph's Church in the 1980s. The church was built on the teachings of Jesus, and enjoyed a reputation of community service for decades. People came from miles around to worship at this popular church.

Mark talked behind Fr. Dunkel's back. He ridiculed him. While Mark didn't draw a line in the sand, he didn't like his priest and most who knew Mark, knew that.

Before Mass on a typical Saturday evening, Mark was asked what he planned to do about getting Fr. Dunkel replaced. He said, loud enough for many to hear, "If I could get him out of St. Joseph's, I'd do it in a

New York minute. This church is doomed as long as the bishop keeps him here. The day he is gone will be one of the happiest days of my life."

As the weeks went on, Mark identified others who seemed to feel the same way. He invited four parishioners to the Miller home to discuss how action could be taken to have Fr. Dunkel removed from St. Joseph's. The four were Mary and Ted Burns and Melody and Jim Atkins.

Following a prayer initiated by Mark, Janet offered a hospitality comment. "Coffee and tea are in the dining room and the aroma you are enjoying is from a batch of chocolate chip cookies which will cool and be ready soon."

"Oh, Janet, I so enjoy your cookies and coffee," Mary Burns replied. "Of course, I believe in our mission and will do my part to right the ship, but if truth be told, I simply love your baking." Others nodded.

"Let's wait till everyone has their refreshments before we begin our discussion," Mark said as members stood to get their food.

Ten minutes later Mark spoke, "I think we're ready to begin. Thank you for coming this evening. We have much to do to plan to take back our church."

"You really think we can pull this off?" Ted Burns asked.

"Absolutely! All we need is the right plan, proper conditions, and a perfect opportunity."

"Melody and I are fairly new to the group," said James Atkins. "Would someone help us understand our mission?"

"That's a good idea, Jim," Mark replied. "Our mission should be clear. Mary, would you please provide the background?"

"Sure. St. Joseph Church was founded in 1976 with a clear mission to advance the good news proclaimed by our Lord and Savior, Jesus Christ, and to create a house of worship that values service to others."

"And, we're gathered this evening because?" Melody asked.

"Our priest, loved as he is by most parishioners, is unworthy to lead St. Joseph's," Mary replied.

"So, we're meeting to rid our church of Father Albert?" Melody asked.

"Janet, these chocolate chip cookies are out of this world," Mary interrupted. "What is your secret?"

"More butter than what is called for, more chips, more sugar, and mix to a good consistency," Janet replied, smiling. She appreciated people who enjoyed her cookies.

"I know the cookies are a hit, Mary, but could we please concentrate on our task at hand?" Ted asked sternly.

Mark brought the group back on task with a bold statement: "Our mission is to rid our church of Fr. Dunkel!"

"Mark, what is your problem?" Jim asked.

"When Father Albert was the pastor of St. John's in Grayling, my nephew Ted Owens was denied going to the seminary because Fr. Dunkel convinced the bishop that he was unfit to be a priest. I was livid. Nobody knows Teddy like I do and Ted would have been a wonderful priest."

"Why? Was a reason ever given?" Melody asked.

"I think he just didn't like people with a disability."

Ted asked, "What was his disability?"

"He dove into a shallow pool when he was a teenager and the injury caused paralysis of his legs."

"I assume he sustained some brain damage?" Mary reasoned.

"No, surprisingly he didn't. I am convinced he would have made a terrific parish priest, but there was one man who stood in the way of his serving the Lord in a most unique way. I am referring to Fr. Dunkel."

"I find it hard to believe," Jim replied. "Everybody, well almost everyone, loves this man. I can't imagine his doing this without a good reason."

"Well, Jim, he did it. I hate him as much as one man can hate another and with this attitude I find other things he says or does to be deplorable."

Melody summarized. "Each of us has reason to want Father replaced, but speaking for the the rest of us, we don't have the intensity of motivation that you have. By being here we respect your mission and join you in your wanting Fr. Dunkel out."

"Thank you!"

So," Jim began. "How do we get rid of Father?"

"There are several ways. We need to find the right one and then execute our plan," Mark replied.

"Execute as in kill him?" Mary asked, aghast.

"Absolutely not," Mark replied. "There is a limit to my desire to rid our church of our priest, but murder is not to happen. The last thing I want to do is break a commandment and commit a mortal sin in the process. If killing proves to be the best option, you can count me out!"

A moment of silence was followed by a comment by Melody Atkins. "Do you think we can pull this off?"

"Absolutely!" Mark fired back. "It has to be planned to perfection. The six of us have superior intelligence and with creative thinking, removing Father from the parish will be a piece of cake."

Ted was skeptical. "Are you thinking of begging the bishop to intervene?"

Mark replied, "That's why we need to talk about, how, where, when, and who."

"Can't we get the bishop to transfer him?" Melody asked.

"How many letters are too many?" Mark asked. "How many visits with the bishop are too many? The bishop's not going to budge. He'll let Father sink with the ship."

"So <u>we</u> need to budge? Is that what you're trying to say?" Ted asked.

"Exactly, if we want to keep him from destroying other lives."

"Why don't we just drop away like others before us who went elsewhere, or better yet, start our own church?" Melody said, not feeling comfortable with the way the meeting was progressing.

"We could but let's not get too dramatic here. We do not want to leave the Catholic Church or lead a protest march to have our church closed. We just need a new priest."

By now, coffee was cool, if not cold; the chosen cookies were eaten with crumbs here and there. "Help yourself to more coffee and then we'll get down to business," Ted suggested.

"Sounds like a plan!" Mark replied.

Chapter Three

Father Albert arrived punctually for his meeting with the bishop. "Thank you for meeting with me."

The bishop nodded. "I'm quite busy but I wanted to listen to your concerns."

"Thank you. I'll only be a few minutes. Bottom line is this—I'm requesting a transfer. I'm not happy and I believe I can be of greater and more effective service to you and God in another setting."

"That's unfortunate," the bishop replied. "As you know we are short on priests. I'm thankful for every one of you."

"Certainly other priests have talked to you about a reassignment."

"Actually, I haven't heard from anyone. Some would undoubtedly welcome a different parish, but it hasn't come to my attention."

"That's surprising," Father Albert replied. "At the last seminar I must've talked with at least six brother priests who wanted to be transferred."

"Tell me, what exactly is making you so unhappy?" the bishop asked.

"I feel that I'm not doing a good job."

"Your congregation loves you, Albert. I get more loving comments about you than all of my priests combined."

"Attendance at St. Joseph's has dropped significantly in the last few years, and we've had no new members for a couple of years now. I've heard a rumor that some of my members want me out and perhaps I am paranoid, but I'm beginning to think they're right."

"Well, there's no truth in that, Albert. But, you haven't given me enough reason to reassign you. I see your depression, but that doesn't warrant reassignment. You need something more substantial."

"Please give me a 'for instance'."

"Mental breakdown, scandal, threat on your life—something significant. You see, an unhappy priest can't compare."

"Well, thanks for meeting with me."

"The Lord's work is never easy, Albert, but the Holy Spirit will guide you."

Fr. Albert felt that the bishop was uncaring and had no interest in helping him. *Guess I need to have a nervous breakdown, initiate a scandal, or have my life threatened*, he thought as he drove out of Cadillac.

Prior to the Tuesday parish council meeting Fr. Albert felt as if he were having a panic attack. His heartbeat quickened, he felt light-headed and nauseated. But, as he had done prior to recent meetings, he resolved to buckle down and get through it. There was always the promise of a few shots of whiskey afterwards.

The parish meeting began at 6:30 p.m. with a prayer from Father Albert. Millie Pritchard, council president, ran a disciplined meeting, sticking to an agenda and promising the meeting would be over in an hour. Most members couldn't decide whether that was because she was obsessive-compulsive, or because a favorite television program was to air at 8:00.

"The first item on the agenda is membership," Millie began. "The bishop expects a certain growth percentage, and as we all know, not only hasn't any member joined recently, but we've lost some families. It appears people would rather go to St. Pat's in Yuma."

"I think it's their youth program," Joan Willems reasoned. "The kids like the youth leader, and they do fun things. The parents are thankful their children want to participate, so they transfer. That way the family can worship together."

"Father, are there any plans to increase membership?" Millie asked.

"No. People who move into the area visit for a Sunday or two, but we don't see them again. I'm sorry. I don't know what to do."

"Well, we can't solve the problem tonight. Let's move to finances. Art, do you have a report?"

"Just more bad news," Art Cantor replied softly. "We can't make payroll. We can't pay down on our mortgage. We can't begin repairs on our roof. Each weekend we take in less and less."

Father interrupted, "I think we should have a campaign to get the money to meet some of these expenses."

"Members are transferring; potential members don't give us more than two weeks. And you can't ask the faithful for more money. It won't work," Art replied.

"Sooner or later, those who have committed to St. Joseph must realize that if they want a church in this town, they need to find the money to meet the expenses."

"I understand, but we risk losing those who are left," Joan pointed out.

"Well, then, maybe it's time to fold," Millie sighed in frustration.

"Or maybe it's time for the bishop to appoint another priest!" Art cried out.

"I'm sorry you feel that way, Art!" Father said as he stood up and walked out of the meeting.

"That was harsh, Art," Millie said, glancing around at the stunned council members.

"I know everyone loves him and so do I, but it had to be said," Art insisted. "I'm sorry if I hurt him, but facing failure is never easy. The bottom line is this: he's not effective; he lacks an understanding of fundraising; and he has poor public-relations skills. I'm afraid that unless we can get him out of the parish, St. Joe's is doomed!"

Millie broke the resulting silence, "In any event, Father is probably disturbed by your comment, Art. You might contact him and apologize."

"I suppose you're right," Art replied.

The next morning, October 11, Father Dunkel met with Delbert Willingham, a parishioner who found comfort in Albert's ministry. Del was wealthy, shy, and a keep-to-himself soul. In reality, he yielded a great deal of influence.

"Del. Thanks for taking time out of your busy day to listen. Perhaps you can offer some advice."

"Anything for you, Father."

"As you know, the parish is on its way to closing. The believers are going elsewhere for a good Catholic education, vibrant youth programs, and a feeling of community. Here, it feels like everyone's sailing with me on the Titanic."

"I've been watching, and each Sunday my heart sinks a bit," Del said sympathetically.

"I met with the bishop and begged to be transferred, but he won't consider it. The situation needs to be much worse for him to make a move."

"Do you want me to call him? He seems to have listened when I've contacted him."

"No, not yet. He said I needed a threat on my life, a scandal, or a nervous breakdown."

"Do you expect to meet any of those conditions?" Del asked.

"No. He would see through it, and I'm not into playing games with my bishop. The long-term implications are complicated."

"So, what will you do?"

"I fear I must allow the parish to fade into oblivion."

"Really?"

"The writing is on the wall. This started long before I was assigned here. You will recall that when I arrived a year ago, finances were not healthy, and the choir had just disbanded. Enrollment in our religious education program was at an all-time low. Granted, I could provide some hope, but the bomb was ticking the day I moved into my office."

"And, the reason you've asked me here?"

"I guess I needed a sounding board. I needed someone who had my back."

"There's nothing you want me to do?" Del asked.

"To be honest, when I asked to meet with you, I had something else on my mind."

"I'm curious."

"Well, maybe I just came to my senses, but I had thought about a staged murder."

"Suicide?"

"Oh, I wouldn't die, but there might be a severe threat to my life."

"How could I help with that?" Del asked, stunned.

"I didn't have a plan. I guess I just needed a friend to hear me out."

"Please don't do anything rash," Del advised. "Call me if you need to talk. Everything will work out for the best. We both believe God has something planned for you. We just don't know what it is yet."

Art called Father the next afternoon. "I'm sorry if I offended you with my comment last evening."

"It caught me off-guard, but after thinking about it, you're right. Another priest might be able to turn things around. I've talked to the bishop about a reassignment, but he won't agree. He says unhappiness is not sufficient reason for a transfer.'"

"The members of the council were concerned that I hurt your feelings. If I did, I'm sorry."

"Nice of you to call, Art. Your comment was a zinger, but I'm not only over it, I agree with you. We can only pray for guidance and try to respond to the Holy Spirit."

The Burns, Atkins, and Millers reconvened the evening of October 15, its members hoping to find a way of bringing a sense of peace and future comfort to the congregation.

As usual, Mark Miller opened the meeting with a prayer, then asked if any member wanted to comment.

Melody started. "I talked to a friend, and she said they have similar issues in their church. They're not willing to take drastic action but some members are concerned and talking."

"You didn't tell her we were planning to rid our parish of our priest, I hope?" Mark asked.

"Oh, gosh, no."

"Did you tell her we meet regularly to discuss a plan?" Mary asked.

"I guess she might have surmised that," she said cringing.

"Listen folks, listen!" Mark insisted. "Nothing must be said about our meetings; what we say, who attends, and what we are planning. All that must never leave this room! If Father's friends, and that is almost everyone in St. Joe's, begin to investigate, they will interview people, and the last thing we need is someone saying, 'I was told about a group disenchanted with their pastor. They met to discuss how they could be rid of him'".

"I didn't put it that way," Melody said, starting to tear up.

"Nothing must be said to anyone about who we are, or what we are planning. Am I clear?"

"I'm sorry if I upset you," Melody replied. "I was just saying…" She wiped her eyes.

"What's done is done. Let's move on. I imagine nothing will come of it."

Melody didn't like what Mark said, nor the tone of his voice. She suddenly wondered if this group was for her. She didn't feel as if she could leave, for the other members might think she would "rat" on them. *I probably would be better off staying with the group,* she thought. *But, this is not where I want to be.*

"We need to set a date for accomplishing our goal," Mark said, getting to the point.

"How about the Sunday after Thanksgiving?" Jim asked. "That gives us planning time."

Janet looked at her smart-phone calendar and replied, "That would be November 27."

"Okay. Is everyone in agreement?" Mark asked. "On or before November 27, our congregation will be free of Father Dunkel. So, let's get to what needs to be done, and by whom. We need to focus energy on a perfect plan."

Chapter Four

With this background we pick up with Michigan detective Lou Searing about to hear of his next case.

Lou Searing raked leaves in front of his home south of Grand Haven. His wife, Carol, was making a Halloween costume for a neighbor. Their cat, Sami Two, slept curled up in an easy chair, while Sami, the golden retriever, watched Lou through the front window, wishing she could romp amidst the colorful leaves.

Lou. who was three weeks into his 75th year, showed all the signs of a senior; bald head, protruding stomach, hearing aids in both ears, and a slower-than-normal gait. But his mind was sharp most of the time, and as Carol would say, he was in pretty good shape for the shape he was in.

Carol presented a contrast, quicker in movement, with perfect hearing, hair cut short, and a quick wit. After 42 years of marriage, they knew each other well enough to know what the other was thinking.

Lou and Carol's home was built on the shore of Lake Michigan, south of Grand Haven. The second floor housed Carol's quilt center, and the next room was Lou's writing studio. Both rooms had large windows, offering wonderful views of the shoreline.

Lou's cell phone, attached to his waist rang. His back was aching so he took the call as a sign to take a break. He didn't recognize the caller or the number.

"Hello."

"Mr. Searing?"

"Yes. Who's calling?"

"This is Stan Kidd, Wexford County Sheriff. We've had a murder in Mesick, and I'm wondering if you can help me."

"Solving a murder is more satisfying than creating piles of leaves on a chilly fall day."

"That's great. My staff could handle it, but a flu bug is going around, plus my lead detective is on leave for a few weeks. Your reputation leads me to think you could solve this crime."

"Have you any of the big four?" Lou asked.

"The big four?"

"Witness, weapon, motive, suspect."

"I can give you two: a witness and a suspect."

"That's a start. Two's better than none."

"If you could drive over, I can tell you everything we know, which isn't much."

"Just to be clear, we're talking about the priest in the Mesick Catholic Church, right?"

"Yes."

"I saw it on CNN earlier today," Lou admitted.

"I didn't know the media outlets had word of this."

"These days, you can't sneeze in a burg without the world hearing about it."

"I guess you're right."

"The media didn't contact you?" Lou asked.

"No, they may have checked in with local police. It's been a zoo around here. Murder is rare in our county, so when it occurs, I guess the world wants to know."

"I'll be over in the morning," Lou said, trying to remember if he had a conflict. "I need to get my wife's blessing. She lives in fear that my demise is on someone's bucket list."

"That's fair. Unless I hear differently, I'll see you in Cadillac tomorrow morning."

"I'll want to go to the scene of the crime."

"That's a given. Let's meet in my office, and then we'll go to Mesick."

"See you tomorrow morning, Sheriff."

Lou put his phone back on his belt and resumed raking.

While Carol prepared dinner—cube steak, mashed potatoes and gravy, along with corn—Lou broached the subject.

"I got a call this noon," he began.

"Where is it this time?" Carol asked, knowing what was coming.

"Wexford County. Did you hear about that priest who was murdered in Mesick? I've been asked to work with Sheriff Kidd to solve it."

"Why does everyone come to you?" Carol asked.

"I've been lucky solving crimes."

"I know you're successful, but why are you the one they always contact?"

"It seems like a lot, but it works out to about one case a year. Believe me, there are dozens of murders each year."

"I know. I just wish you'd retire so I don't have to start planning your funeral every time you take on a case."

Lou was surprised. "That's pretty negative, coming from you."

"You're right," Carol replied. "It's a crazy world out there. By now, I imagine that if a murderer knows you're on the case, knocking you off is about his or her only chance of not being caught. You're a major threat to every murderer you investigate. Odds are pretty high that your life's on the line."

"I see your point," Lou sighed. "If you don't want me to go, I won't."

"I want you to be happy," Carol said. "If solving these murders makes you happy and fulfilled, by all means pursue your passion. I shouldn't stand in your way, but I do appreciate your seeking my thoughts before heading out to slay the windmills."

"I'll be careful. How about this? I'll hang it up after this one, okay?"

Carol laughed and hugged him. "You'll <u>never</u> hang it up, Lou. It's who you are, your reason for being. It's me who needs to adjust, and I will."

Lou arrived at the county sheriff's office at 8:42 the next morning, October 31. Sheriff Kidd was waiting for him with hot coffee in hand. They proceeded to a conference room and sat at a large table.

"Thanks for the coffee, Sheriff. Tell me what you know about this crime. I'll take notes."

"The victim is Father Albert Dunkel, sixty-one years old. The priesthood was his second career following a physics professorship at Notre Dame. Our best guess is he was shot by a man in the front pew, about fifteen feet from where he stood during Mass. It made for lots of confusion as you can imagine. People were stunned. Some knelt and prayed, but most went outside. Obviously, the shooter walked out.

"I'm told that people did not expect murder. They thought Father had fainted. So, while there was concern, there was no panic. A doctor immediately went to Father, but she kept a cool head and didn't tell anyone he had been shot."

"No witnesses?" Lou asked.

"In a sense, everyone in the sanctuary was a witness. But the only one who thought she saw a gun was Mrs. Bosseker, the organist. She and Father were the only two facing the congregation."

"No altar servers?" Lou asked, knowing the Mass routine, himself a Catholic.

"Thank goodness, no. The kids were on a retreat."

"What's the priest's reputation?" Lou asked.

"Everyone loves him is what I hear."

"Have you gone through his office and home?"

"We've cordoned them off, but I really wanted you here first."

"Thanks. Who do I speak with for parish information?"

"I've heard from Bishop Grether," Sheriff Kidd explained. "Fr. Richards from St. Pat's in Yuma will be available to assist us."

"I'll need to contact him."

"Sure. Anything else you need?"

"Protocol. Does the bishop know I'm working on your behalf? Also, who is the church secretary and will anyone think twice seeing me roaming about?"

"The secretary is Mrs. Hoffman. If anyone seems concerned with your work, have them contact me."

"Thanks, Sheriff."

"How will you begin?" Sheriff Kidd asked.

"I'll talk to Father Richards. Then I want to go through the victim's office and living quarters. I'll need to talk to his staff too."

"Mrs. Hoffman is making arrangements."

The phone rang and the sheriff answered. After listening to the caller, Sheriff Kidd said, "You'll have to talk to Lou Searing. He's responsible for the investigation. Would you like to speak with him? Hold on."

Lou took the phone, covered the microphone, and asked, "Who's this?"

"Newspaper reporter." Lou nodded and then spoke into the phone. "This is Lou Searing."

"Alex Halley, *Traverse City Record-Eagle*. Have you a suspect in Father Dunkel's murder?"

"A suspect? Not yet. I've just been briefed."

"How can I work with you?" Alex asked.

"Stay out of my way, get your facts straight, check out all rumors before going to print. Do that and you'll stay on my good side."

"I follow. We're going to get along well."

The two traded contact information. When Lou hung up, he looked at the sheriff, "Is that guy OK?"

"I've had no trouble with him. He's been around a long time and knows how to work with us. You'll find him a good guy."

"He'd better be. One slip and he's off my radar. I don't have time for rookies or know-it-alls."

"While you were on the phone, I contacted Fr. Richards in Yuma. He'll meet you at St, Joseph's in Mesick. Ready to head over there?"

Lou pulled up at the rectory of St. Joseph's. Father Richards, pastor at St. Pat's in Yuma was tall and distinguished-looking. He was waiting out front. He sported a white goatee and a sincere smile. Lou and Father Richards walked the church grounds. They stopped outside the garage. The one-car garage was locked but they could see a car through a window. "Later I'll want to search that car," Lou said.

"You're the boss," Father Richards agreed.

"So, I take it, you now have two parishes to administer," Lou said, making light conversation.

"Yes, the bishop asked me to substitute for Fr. Dunkel. Once you've cleared it, I plan to use his office when I'm here."

"Let's take a look around."

They found the office well-organized and without clues. Lou found nothing unusual in Albert's appointment book.

"Have you been in his living quarters?"

"No."

The two then walked to the rectory next to the church. Nothing inside the small apartment indicated a struggle or that anything was amiss. No notes were found.

"Not much here," Father Richards said. The two walked into the church, unlocked the door to the sacristy, entered, but found nothing that related to the crime.

Chapter Five

Lou's cell phone rang.

"Lou, this is Sheriff Kidd."

"I trust you have some news."

"For what it's worth, I got a call from Halley, the *Record-Eagle* reporter. He said he'd heard a rumor about a guy planning to kill his pastor in Mesick. He wouldn't give me his source, figuring passing along the tip was favor enough."

"Who's plotting this death?"

"He didn't say, but the plot is supposedly being hatched by a small group of members at St. Joseph's."

"Ok. Thanks for the call. I'll let you know if I learn anything."

Lou didn't waste time in calling Alex. "I understand you have some information about the priest's murder?"

"Yeah, I got a call from someone who had read my latest article. I called the sheriff to brief him."

"I know. He passed it along, but I'd like more specific information."

"That's it. I don't know any more."

Lou sensed he wasn't getting the whole story. "Listen Alex, we can be a good team, or we can play the 'I'm keeping this to myself' game. If you expect a breaking headline once this is solved, I expect you to give me <u>all</u> the facts."

"Fair enough. The man's name is Mark Miller. He heads a small committee who wanted to rid their church of its pastor, or priest, I guess. I'm told Miller will be arrested soon."

"Arrested by whom?" Lou asked. "The sheriff has jurisdiction. He would tell me before he considers an arrest."

"The state police are in on the tip, but I don't know how they're working with Sheriff Kidd. The MSP detective is Sergeant Powers. I'll give you his number."

"Thanks, Alex."

Lou called Detective Powers. "I'm Lou Searing, working with Sheriff Kidd on the priest murder. I understand you have a suspect in mind, if not in custody?"

"That's correct. We're in touch with Sheriff Kidd."

"Can you tell me what's going on?"

"I'll need to verify that you're working with the sheriff."

"I understand. Again, my name is Lou Searing. Once you get clearance, I would appreciate a call telling me what you know."

"I'll be back with you presently, Mr. Searing."

"Thank you, Detective."

Within ten minutes Detective Powers called back. "Mr. Searing? I've talked to Sheriff Kidd, and he okayed sharing information with you."

"Good."

"We got a tip a few hours ago that a subject by the name of Mark Miller was plotting the demise of his pastor. Miller lives in Mesick. He wasn't at home and his wife didn't know or wouldn't tell us his whereabouts. We put out a 'Be on the Lookout Bulletin', and his vehicle was spotted about 15 miles east on M-42. When we pulled him over, he wasn't cooperative."

"Did you arrest him?"

"No, we didn't have cause. We advised him to contact his lawyer and to stay in the area."

"What was his response?"

"He denied everything including planning to remove his pastor. He was almost uncontrollably angry that we pulled him over, said he was going to call his lawyer and press charges for harassment. He was a real hot-head."

"But, he was free to go."

"That's right. We have the encounter on the cam in my vehicle. He didn't break any laws but one might be hard-pressed to call him innocent. He didn't act like a normal person."

The next day, Tuesday, November 1, Lou learned from the sheriff that Mark Miller had been arrested because the church organist was quite certain he was the man she saw in the front row of the church.

He wouldn't, or couldn't, provide an alibi regarding his whereabouts at the time of the murder. He also changed his story and admitted he was a part of a group that wanted to replace his pastor.

"Circumstantial, Sheriff," Lou said.

"I agree, but the judge felt the prosecutor was convincing, so Miller's being held in the county jail."

"Did he post bail?"

"The judge wouldn't allow it based on his behavior when we pulled him over."

Later the same morning, Lou asked to speak with the Reverend John Grether, the bishop of the diocese of Northwest Michigan. He found time to see Lou.

"I'm sorry for your loss, Bishop," Lou began.

"Thank you. I'm grateful you'll be investigating this horrific crime."

"I'll do the best I can. As I begin, please tell me what you know."

"I know that Fr. Dunkel was not happy in Mesick. When he asked me to transfer him, I told him unhappiness was not a sufficient reason to be reassigned."

"What would it take for a reassignment, Bishop?"

"I told him a scandal, a threat on his life, or a mental health issue."

"Did he seem so unhappy that he might try to create one of these situations?"

"I didn't have that sense, but it would be consistent with his personality. Albert was always complaining about this or that. I get a request from him for reassignment about every four months. I could almost set my calendar by his requests to meet. Each time, he wasn't happy. I'd deny the request and he'd be on his way, only to return later with the same song, different verse."

"Did a parishioner ever talk with you about his being a problem?"

"I got a letter or two from a couple of disgruntled members. Parishioners usually talk by their actions. They simply up and leave. Fighting the system is rarely successful. It's much easier to walk to another parish, or in some instances, to another denomination. What makes this odd is that Fr. Dunkel is loved by his parishioners. He's the most popular priest ever to serve at St. Joe's."

"Has anyone ever been brought to your attention because of violent tendencies?"

"Every diocese has its share of mentally-ill people. So, yes, I am concerned about a few, and you can get their names from Sheriff Kidd."

"I need their names as soon as possible," Lou said emphatically.

"Very well. My secretary will get that for you before you leave."

"Thank you. One more question. Did anyone call your office with information or just to talk about Father's murder?"

"We got a few sympathy cards. I'll ask my secretary, but she didn't tell me of a call or a request to visit."

"As this investigation unfolds, do I contact you, or a designee?"

"I would rather you contact me," Bishop Grether replied.

Chapter Six

While Lou had met Father Richards and toured St. Joseph's church with him, he hadn't interviewed him, so he made plans to do so. Lou returned to Mesick on Wednesday, November 2.

"Fr. Richards, I understand you and Fr. Dunkel were good friends."

"Yes, we were. We went through seminary together and were ordained at the same time."

"Is it fair to say, that no one knows Father Albert better than you, at least within the past few years?"

"Other than his mother, I would think I'm it."

"I need to learn as much about Fr. Albert as possible. If you don't mind, I'll record what you say so I can take notes and study your comments later."

"Fine."

I want to know interests, hobbies, habits. Also, if there are any skeletons in the closet, I need to know those as well."

"I'll tell you what I know."

"Okay, I'll turn on my recorder and you tell me about your friend.

I'll interrupt if I need something additional or if I need you to clarify."

"It's hard to know where to start, so I'll start with when we met. We were introduced to each other at a bishop's reception for men thinking of the priesthood. We connected because we were about the same age, and most of the men were much younger. We were considering becoming priests after many years in another career, he in university teaching, and me in business.

"My initial reaction was he was a nice guy. I enjoyed his sense of humor. He was intelligent, and we enjoyed some serious conversations about politics, world events, and religion. He liked whiskey, and I enjoyed scotch, so we shared a liking of spirits. He didn't smoke, but I did, a pipe—oral fixation, I guess.

"You asked about skeletons in the closet. He had a short fuse. I don't know if that's a skeleton or simply an aspect of his personality. If something didn't go his way, or the way he thought it should go, he got upset."

"Give me an example," Lou stated.

"Here's one. The women of the parish wanted to have a wild game dinner. Albert didn't think this was appropriate, and he just came unglued, talked loud and looked quite angry, which he was. He later told me he was embarrassed at how he acted, but believed his words and actions were justified, in that he felt people should work to protect wildlife not shoot it."

"Did the women have the dinner?"

"No. They were at loggerheads, and the women shut down the event, which meant some charities missed out on thousands of dollars. But, that's an example of a skeleton."

"I understand."

"This was a rare example. He loved the women's organization and they, him. It was beautiful to see mutual respect. But, as I've said, if he doesn't agree, he can show a different side of his personality.

"On the other side of the coin, he had a great bedside presence. He was very compassionate with the sick, those confined to home, the poor. His heart was welcoming. I would say that aspect of his personality was his gift.

"He was a baseball fan. I went to a game with him once. If an umpire's call was not to his liking, he would light into him. It was embarrassing listening to him carrying on like that. I didn't go with him after that.

"He sat on the traditional side of the aisle, to use a political analogy. He didn't like many of the reforms of Vatican II. He was raised in a traditional parish by strict parents, and that produced a strict traditional priest."

"Another example, please."

"Girls were not allowed to be altar servers. Altar serving represented a small step toward becoming a priest, and since girls were not on the way to priesthood, why tease them with a taste of someday being the celebrant on the altar?"

"Could women be Eucharistic ministers or readers?" Lou asked.

"At first no, but when the church women made quite a scene about being rejected, Father Albert relented. I mean, they carried placards on the sidewalk every Sunday before Mass. The community got involved; the newspaper editor reported the issue, so Father took a beating in the local paper. He eventually gave in and allowed women to participate. But, as you can imagine from earlier personality statements, he lost control with his tongue. It was ugly, but he was a man of principle, and he got his way, one way or another.

"Having said this, his parishioners loved him. Oh sure, there were a couple of negative people. Every parish has them, but again, in spite of a show of disapproval on occasion, he was loved and respected."

"What about his career before becoming a priest?" Lou asked.

"I don't know much. He was a professor, and I think he was respected. He did say once that he was frustrated because he wanted to do research, but he couldn't secure grants for the physics department. He basically taught undergraduate classes, and he did some work with Ph.D. candidates. He also served on thesis committees for master's degree candidates."

"Why did he leave the university?"

"He never said."

"Did he have tenure?"

"I don't know."

"As far as you know, he was not fired."

"Correct."

"Where was he a professor?"

"Notre Dame."

"The department was…?

"Physics."

"Oh yes, you mentioned that. Go on with your description of him."

"Well, he didn't like to cook. He ate all of his meals in local restaurants or at church events. He would make chocolate brownies, but that was it.

"He didn't like television. It's a waste of one's brain, he'd say. However, he went to a lot of movies—which to me is glorified television. I like television. It's a relaxer for me.

"He was a member of the local Lions Club. He went to the meeting every Tuesday noon—another meal provided for a fee. He liked the programs and he liked serving the community.

"Oh, yeah, he was quite a crossword-solver. He'd get the *Detroit Free Press* and, if he had the time, he'd solve all three crossword puzzles.

He told me he did crossword puzzles while in the confessional, waiting for parishioners to come to confession. Not many went to him because, I'm told, he was harsh, if you know what I mean. So, he had a lot of quiet time in his confessional, a perfect setting to work on his crossword puzzles."

Lou nodded. "One more question: in your interaction with Fr. Albert, did he ever say he feared someone or had had a run-in with anyone?"

Father Richards paused. "He never said he feared anyone, nor did he believe his style of ministry would lead to violence."

"Okay, thanks a lot, Father. I'm going to talk to the Grand Knight this evening and I'll probably talk to the dean of the physics department at Notre Dame. In the meantime, if you think of something else that would help me understand your friend, please contact me."

"Absolutely."

The Grand Knight of the St. Joseph Council was Tony Zuidema.

"Zuidema sounds like a Dutch name," Lou began. "Seems to me you'd be Dutch Reformed."

"I'm a convert. I met my wife in high school. She was Catholic and wouldn't marry me unless I converted. That seemed like a pretty simple thing to do to win her hand as well as her parent's approval so I joined. At the time, I wasn't going to any church. I was baptized in the Reformed Church, but I just wasn't into Sunday school, youth group, any of that stuff. Mary Ann came with a religion. It was 'Love me, love my church,' so I did—a small price to pay for eternal happiness."

"Everyone has an interesting story."

"Yes. They do. Are you Catholic?"

"Not a 'cradle Catholic.' Like you, I'm a convert, and it was my second wife, Carol, who influenced me. Before you ask, I'm a member of the Knights, and over the years I've served in most offices. I was even in the 4th Degree Color Corps for several years."

"Well, we are bonded in our Catholicism," Tony said. "What can I do for you?"

"I'm trying to figure out who killed Fr. Dunkel."

"Terrible, terrible tragedy."

"Was he a Knight?"

"Oh yes, he rarely missed a meeting. He worked alongside us at our events; pancake breakfasts, annual car show and I could go on, but you get the idea."

"Who do you think killed him?" Lou asked.

"It wasn't Mark Miller—the guy in jail at the moment."

"And you say this because?" Lou urged Tony to continue.

"Because he had no motive. I know Mark. Not well, but I know of him, and he's innocent. He's going to sue somebody and get millions. I'm very respectful of our law enforcement, but thankfully they have little, if any, experience with murder. They just heard the organist say it was Mark Miller, and when he couldn't, or wouldn't, give an alibi, they arrested him."

"Then who do you think shot him?" Lou asked, pen in hand.

"I'm confident that when all is said and done, the murderer will not be a member of this parish."

"You may be right. Time will tell."

"That's what is so baffling to me," Tony mused. "Why would anyone stand in front of a couple hundred people and shoot a priest? Remember when Jack Ruby shot Oswald on TV? You saw people jump him immediately. Why wasn't this guy jumped right after the shot, or certainly on his way out of the building? Either the guy wanted to be caught, or he was mentally ill."

"It's puzzling," Lou admitted. "Did anybody hate Father?"

"Those who were traditionalists thought he was a gift from God. He represented pre-Vatican II changes. Fr. Dunkel gave them hope that one day the Catholic church would return to the old days. Back when Mass was in Latin, women wore head-coverings, everyone knelt for most of the Mass, and only those in a state of grace without mortal sin could take communion."

"I guess I'm finished here. Thanks for speaking with me."

"Leave your business card so I can contact you if I need to. Thank you for working on this case. We know you'll solve it, you always do."

"Thank you."

Before heading home to Grand Haven, Lou contacted Mrs. Miller. Janet invited Lou into her home and seemed to welcome the opportunity to talk with him.

"This must be a very stressful time for the Miller family," Lou began.

"Yes, quite unnerving."

"Are you getting along okay?'

"Yes. We know Mark didn't do this. He wasn't in church the weekend of Father's murder."

"Mrs. Bosseker remains adamant that he was in the front row."

"Did she have her glasses on?" Janet asked.

"I don't know."

"She wears glasses to read the music but if she is looking at something beyond ten feet or so, whatever she sees is blurred."

"Interesting. Does Mark ever sit in the first row?"

"Often. That raises another thing. We never go to the Sunday morning Mass. We are loyal Saturday evening parishioners."

Lou took copious notes. "You said Mark wasn't in church the weekend Father Albert was killed. Where was he?"

"I can't say. Mark would be upset if I explained. It would break a confidence."

"So he wasn't in church and you won't say where he was that morning."

"Yes."

"I'm confused; explaining would free your husband," Lou said

"This is something that will have to come from Mark. I can't comment."

"Here is my card. Please contact me if there is anything you wish to ask or share. How is your daughter handling all of this?"

"Wonderfully. Charlene knows her father is innocent. The kids at school and in our neighborhood have been supportive."

"That's good. Thanks for talking with me. I'll be on my way."

Chapter Seven

On his way from Mesick to Grand Haven, Lou called his prime source of information and advice, Jack Kelly. Jack, with his mother, Elaine, lives in Muskegon, Michigan. He has worked with Lou for seven or eight years. He was a whiz at getting the information Lou needed to solve a crime. At 53, Jack is a volunteer at his church and often goes on church missions to help those in poverty.

"Jack, I have another case, and I need your help."

"That priest near Yuma? I read about that in the paper."

"That's the one. I need whatever you can find about Albert Dunkel. He was a professor of physics at Notre Dame, but for some reason, he walked away from that job and joined a seminary. He's been a priest for less than 10 years, and his last parish was St. Joseph's in Mesick."

"Okay, I have my marching orders. When do you need this?" Jack asked. "I'm pretty busy at the moment, but for you, I usually drop everything."

"I appreciate it, but I'm not in a big hurry. I'd like something within a few days, but I trust you'll get to it when you can."

"I'll get on it, Lou. Talk to you soon."

"Give my best to Elaine."

"I will. Thanks, Lou."

Lou learned that the chair of the physics department at Notre Dame in South Bend was Dr. Dick Reed. When Lou called he was told that Dr. Reed could see him as soon as he got to campus, so Lou drove from Cadillac to South Bend.

Once they were seated in Dr. Reed's office, Lou began. "Thanks for meeting me on short notice."

"Our priorities are the same," Dr. Reed replied. "What do you need?"

"As you may have heard, Father Albert Dunkel was murdered while celebrating Mass recently."

"Yes, we've heard. A tragic loss of life. Albert was a gifted person."

"I'm here to learn as much as possible about this man. As you can imagine, I'm looking for any conflicts in his life."

"With students?" Dr. Reed asked.

"With anyone. Who in his life was problematic? A student, a class, another professor, a dean, a coach, a president, a priest? It seems there's no end to who might have rubbed Albert the wrong way or vice versa."

"Actually only a couple of confrontations come to mind, both having to do with Ph.D. committees. In both instances, a Ph.D. candidate was defending a dissertation when both of their career paths took a terrible turn."

"This is exactly what I'm looking for," Lou replied, taking notes. "Please go on."

"Several years ago, two students researched string theory for their dissertations."

"What does that mean, professor?" Lou asked.

String theory is a set of attempts to model the four known fundamental interactions; gravitation, electromagnetism, strong nuclear force, weak nuclear force—together in one theory. This tries to resolve the alleged conflict between classical physics and quantum physics by elementary units—the one classical force: gravity, and a new quantum field theory of the other three fundamental forces.

"Stop right there. This is going to be way over my head."

"Trust me. It's a theory that some scientists believe explains the make up of the universe. Anyway, Dr. Dunkel considered string theory ridiculous. So, when a Ph.D. candidate sought the degree based on research in that controversial area, Dr. Dunkel refused to vote to grant the candidate the degree."

"You mean, after years of study and research, these two were denied the degree?" Lou asked, seeking clarification.

"Yes, but it meant a lot more than the degree, since they couldn't get a job where an advanced degree was a prerequisite. The sad part of the story is that the research was valid. Prestigious journals were ready to publish the work, but when the candidates didn't pass their orals, there was no degree, and hence, no published work. The candidates were devastated. They saw their futures in research or university teaching come crashing down."

"There was no appeal?" Lou asked.

"The voting by the orals committee is final. However, the candidate can write a new dissertation, based on a new hypothesis. Neither candidate chose this route."

"What happened to the candidates?"

"The first was Jennifer Kale who never got over it. She fell into severe depression and had to be hospitalized. She just disappeared from our radar. I don't know what became of her."

"And the other?"

"The other was Tyrone Babcock. I don't know what happened to him, either."

"So, Dunkel simply left Notre Dame? Did he have a choice? Were you the Chair of the department back then?"

"No, I wasn't. Harriet Stocker was Dean then. There was an effort to rescind Dr. Dunkel's tenure, but lawyers for Albert were successful in suppressing the attempt. He was basically shunned by his colleagues. They made his academic life miserable. He resigned in 2010."

"And, he decided to become a priest."

"Yes. Between you and me, I was shocked that he was accepted into the seminary. I couldn't believe an admissions committee would allow a man with such extreme narcissism to enter a profession requiring exceptional social skills, most of which Dunkel sorely lacked."

"Do you have any contact information for Tyrone Babcock?"

"I don't."

"You don't have a file with correspondence, or a personnel file?"

"Tyrone and Notre Dame agreed to destroy all personal information kept by the University. Further, the University agreed not to share written or verbal information about Tyrone with anyone for a period of twenty-five years. I suppose I shouldn't have told you anything."

"Situational ethics, Professor," Lou replied. "I need your knowledge to investigate a homicide. Whether sharing is 'legal' or not, a judge would expect you to work with investigators. If Tyrone complains, we'll work with the prosecutor to absolve you of any blame. In this case, you were placed between a rock and a hard place."

"Really, I have no concerns."

"I'll leave you to your work. I thank you for your time and information."

Before Lou left campus, he called Jack.

"I've a couple more people for you to research. The first is Tyrone Babcock, a Ph.D. candidate at Notre Dame in 2005. He was denied a Ph.D. in physics because of Albert's opinion of his research topic. The second is Jennifer Kale. She also was denied a Ph.D. degree when the orals committee rejected her work."

"I'll get on it. While you're on the line, I've found something on your victim, Father Dunkel. He was raised in South Haven, and he has one entry in a police record. While he was in high school, he threatened his scoutmaster because he denied Albert the rank of Eagle Scout. The scoutmaster didn't press charges, since he understood Albert's anger."

"How was the scoutmaster threatened?" Lou asked.

"Albert was concocting a poison to put into a soda can, but a friend learned of the plan and called police. Nothing happened, but Albert was detained, and as a condition to have the crime report expunged from his record, he needed to get psychiatric counseling. However, he only attended one session, so his police record stands."

"Thanks, Jack. I'm on my way home. Let's have coffee sometime next week."

"I'd like that."

Sheriff Kidd called Lou as he approached the Grand Haven city limits. "CSI has found something of interest in Father Dunkel's office file."

"What is that?"

"A letter to Albert from a Jennifer Kale. She wrote a damning letter ending with a threat. I quote: 'I assure you that, just as you ruined my career in my chosen profession, I will end your chosen career. How ironic that you're now a priest, representing Jesus Christ. Jesus mixed with the alienated of society. You fit right in. As the saying goes, 'Live your life looking over your shoulder, because when you least expect it, I'll enjoy taking revenge for your despicable behavior.'"

"When is the letter dated?" Lou asked.

"February 14, 2012."

"Some valentine, huh? Is there a return address?"

"No."

"How about a postmark on the envelope?"

"I can see a couple of numbers, but not the full zip code."

"Ask the state police crime lab to study the postmark, and then let me know the code when they find it. Did she sign the letter?"

"Yes."

"Good, we'll need to assure that the signature is hers, because once we talk to her, if she becomes a viable suspect, that letter will become a wild card in our hand. Also, see if the lab can detect any fingerprints on the stationery and envelope."

"Will do."

"Did you find anything else?"

"That's it. This Jennifer could be our killer. At least it's something to go on."

"I'll ask Jack Kelly to find her. He's fast, so I may have her located before your lab deciphers the zip code."

The Committee of six met at the Miller home on November 5. Melody and Jim Atkins were unable to meet. As usual, they opened with a prayer and then enjoyed refreshments.

Janet, Mary and Ted Burns were quiet and subdued. There was no official second-in-command but Mary Burns seemed to accept the mantle of leadership. "I can't believe Mark's in jail. There's no way he would kill a priest!"

"How can you say that, Mary?" Ted offered. "He led our efforts to rid our parish of Father. Anyone with a mindset to take threatening action can kill someone. By chairing this committee, he carried a brand that says, 'I commit to ridding our parish of this man'."

"You've a point there," Mary replied. "I still refuse to believe that Mark had anything to do with the priest's death."

"All the evidence is circumstantial from what I've read in the newspaper and heard on television," Ted stated. "He's in trouble because he can't prove he wasn't at Mass the morning Father was shot."

"I've heard that the police know he led our group, intending to remove Father," Mary said. "How could they have known that?"

"It had to be Melody Atkins!" Ted exclaimed.

"Just when you think you can trust people to keep a secret, the secret is out," Mary said.

"Let's not collapse in mistrust. We need to support Mark and renew our vow of silence," Ted said. Everyone nodded.

"I think we should disband," Janet Miller suggested. "We can't continue to meet. One thing at a time. We need to concentrate on getting Mark free. People are talking, while many say our group is just a product of gossip and don't believe such a thing could exist, others think there's some truth to the rumor. We can't give anyone any reason to give the gossip credibility."

"I agree, "Mary replied. "This committee is, as of this moment, non-existent. If the question ever comes up, we say such a committee was never formed, and no plan for anyone's demise was discussed."

"To do otherwise is to keep Mark as a prime suspect and put ourselves in jeopardy," Janet said.

The group immediately changed face. From that moment on, the group became a Bible study group who had been studying Cain's murder of his brother, Abel.

The group didn't realize that media representatives were monitoring the Miller house. As members of the "Bible study" left the house, their photos were taken. The group was now public knowledge.

As Janet approached her car, a news reporter caught up to her. "Can you tell me about this group?"

"It's Bible study. What's all this commotion? Can't a group of Christians hold a Bible study in a home anymore?"

"Rumor has it that you're part of a conspiracy to kill your priest."

"Oh, give me a break! How far from reality can you be? We're discussing Cain's murder of his brother, Abel, and how society really hasn't changed much. Killing our priest is nonsense. Excuse me." Janet got into her car and drove away.

At the same time, another reporter was talking with Mary. "Is your group involved in the murder of the priest?"

"Absurd," Mary replied. "We're a church of love and respect for each other. Once they get to the bottom of this, you'll see that this is a huge misunderstanding."

Chapter Eight

On Saturday, November 6, Jack called Lou. "That zip code is 48660, and I was able to verify the name as Jennifer Kale. She lives alone at One Pine Grove Avenue in Midland. She has a clean police record. She attends the St. Luke Catholic Church and is quite active with St. Vincent de Paul and in their program to help the homeless. Jennifer doesn't sound like a murderer, but a lot of sweet little old ladies who supposedly wouldn't swat a fly are now in a womens' prison."

"Do you have a phone number for Jennifer?"

"Only a cell phone. I'm texting it."

"Thanks, Jack. Good work!"

Lou didn't waste a minute. He called Jennifer, explained his purpose in calling, and asked to meet with her.

"This is about that dead priest, isn't it?" Jennifer asked.

"Yes. I understand you knew him when you were a student at Notre Dame."

"Yeah, I did. Terrible professor, and a terrible human being. I guess the Catholic Church takes anybody these days."

"I'd like to talk to you in person."

"I didn't kill him, if that's what you want to ask. Believe me, I wished him dead, but while I'd like some heavy revenge; I've no desire to spend years locked up in some women's prison. I may not be the sharpest knife in the drawer, but I'm not stupid."

"As I said, I want your experience of this man. May I meet with you?"

"Sure, it's a waste of your time, but if you want to talk with me, come to Midland."

"Is tomorrow morning okay with you?"

"I go to 8 a.m Mass, so I can see you after nine o'clock."

"Thank you. Shall we meet at the church? Or, if there's a coffee shop close by, we could meet there."

"Call me when you arrive, and I'll suggest a place." Jennifer replied.

"Fine. Thank you, Miss Kale."

Lou called Jennifer when he entered the city limits of Midland. "Let's meet at the Coffee Spoon on Dow Avenue downtown," she suggested.

"I'll be there shortly. Thanks."

Over coffee and muffins, Lou began work on his mission for the day. "You had a terrible disagreement with Professor Dunkel at Notre Dame."

"Yes, I did. He was on my doctoral committee and initiated a 'no' vote following my oral exam, where I defended my dissertation. According to my advisor, this exercise was simply a formality, because the research I had done was excellent. All the known criticisms were accounted for. I had been told that, once my research was published in a reputable journal, I could be on my way to a prestigious faculty position at MIT, or anywhere for that matter."

"That was it? One 'no' vote by a prof, and you fail your orals?"

"He convinced the other members of my committee that my research was flawed. This was because of jealousy, in that his research was inferior to my work."

"There ought to be some system of appeal," Lou offered.

"Oh, there is, but the power of the professor standing behind academic freedom allowed the department chairs, the Dean, and the Vice President for Academic Affairs to support this jerk."

"This must have given you years of bitterness, anger, and frustration," Lou acknowledged.

"And thoughts of murder, if truth be told."

"Do you know Tyrone Babcock?" Lou asked. "I understand he went through a similar hell."

"Yeah, we're bonded in our hatred of Dunkel."

"So, have you two connected?"

"We e-mail each other and have met a couple of times to put a curse on Dunkel. We even bought a voodoo doll and spent an evening sticking pins in the doll's heart, hoping somehow the spirit would act out our symbolism."

"Looks like it worked," Lou said. "Somebody ended his life."

"Karma," Jennifer explained. "The only problem is, he didn't suffer for years like we did."

"I need to get right to the point. You said you didn't kill him. Did Tyrone kill him?"

"I don't know. I don't think so. He's an intelligent guy. If he was behind it, he wouldn't shoot Dunkel in a crowded church. A man of his intelligence would come up with an ingenious means of murder to keep himself off the suspect list."

"Did he ever say that he planned to kill Dunkel?"

"Actually, I'm the one who talked about killing him. Tyrone would listen, smile, give me fist-bumps, but he never encouraged me, or said to leave it to him."

"Do you know of anyone besides you that talked of taking his life?"

"No."

"How can I contact Ty?"

"He lives in Caro, in the thumb. I'm sure he'd be willing to talk with you. I think he adjusted fairly well."

"Have you a phone number for him?"

"Yes, I'll give it to you before you go."

Lou continued with his questions. "Who were the profs on your dissertation committee?"

There were three: Dunkel, Dr. Nix, and one more, but I don't remember his name. He was a namby-pamby, smart, but no backbone. He would do whatever Dunkel wanted."

"One last question. Were there other students who passed their orals and received the degrees when you were at Notre Dame?"

"There was a lady, a Mrs. Kozminski. I think she died. She was much older than the rest of us, a sister-in-law of the chair of the chemistry department. Dunkel was probably afraid he'd be hung from the closest oak if he voted her out."

"Lou gathered his notes. Thank you for your help. Please contact me if you think of anything to add. Here's my card."

"You're really talking to the wrong person. If I ever hear who killed Dunkel, the last person I would tell is you! I'd do everything I could to help him or her maintain his or her freedom. I would owe that person a huge debt of gratitude."

"I understand, but I sense you're one who would want justice."

"I'm going to confession after our meeting. I'm sure I haven't sounded forgiving or non-judgmental. I don't pray for my enemies and I don't turn the other cheek. My God, get me to the confessional!"

Lou thanked Jennifer, paid the bill, and walked to his car with plenty to think about.

Lou called Ty Babcock, explained who he was, and asked to interview him. Ty was willing to talk, and he had time, so Lou began.

"That negative vote for you in passing your orals must have been a terrible experience."

"Oh yeah, huge disappointment."

"Did you harbor any feelings of revenge?"

Ty sighed. "At first I did. I wanted to fight city hall, but a lawyer I respected calmed me down. He said I had practically no chance of reversing the decision, so I should get on with my life. I talked to Jennifer Kale, too. Have you met her?"

"Yes. I've talked to Jennifer."

"It really threw her for a loop. She had some major mental health problems as a result of the rejection. Gradually, I came to accept it as a life lesson, and I did as my lawyer suggested; I found my angel, got married, and then discovered a niche of teaching physics to home-schoolers."

"If you were in my shoes, who do you think could murder Dunkel?"

Lou asked.

"Obviously I don't know, or I'd tell you. Having said that, if I were a betting man, I'd suspect Tim O'Shaughnessy. Dunkel convinced the committee to can him as well. Neither Jennifer nor I reached out to him once the ax fell. To be honest we were kind of scared of him."

"Why?"

"An odd duck. He was a nice guy, don't get me wrong, but he was a bit off-center. If the truth be known, Jennifer and I thought he wasn't worthy of the degree. We didn't think his research held up. We actually felt sorry for him. He didn't have a close friend. The stress of being a doctoral student seemed to wear on him. When you finish your investigation, it would not shock me if Tim was the guilty one."

"You seem to have adjusted to this quite well," Lou summarized.

"Thank you. What I experienced I wouldn't wish on an enemy, but you can't go through life being bitter. It didn't seem justified, but people face things every day that don't seem fair."

"Thanks for talking with me, Ty."

"Contact me again if you think I can help."

Lou called Jack and reported on his conversation with Ty Babcock. Lou asked if Jack could locate and obtain a copy of Mrs. Kozminski's dissertation from the Notre Dame Library. Once he had it, Jack said he would send it to Lou electronically. Jack found it with no problem. The research was titled, "The Faulty Reasoning of the String Theory." Lou looked at the study on his computer.

Lou had asked Jack for the entire dissertation, but all he really needed was the names of the orals committee, which would be found in the acknowledgements section of the thesis. As predicted, these read: "Sincere thanks are extended to my dissertation committee: Dr. Dunkel, Chair; Dr. Nix; and Dr. Winslow for their guidance, their patience, and their vast knowledge of theories of the structure of the universe."

Lou thanked Jack via e-mail for the file and asked him to locate Dr. Nix and Dr. Winslow.

A few hours later, Jack called. Dr. Nix has been granted a sabbatical for one academic year; he is a full professor in the Physics Department of Boston College, free to come and go as he wishes. His main responsibility is to mentor graduate students and to monitor research in his field of expertise.

Dr. Winslow had retired in 2014 from NASA where he was a consultant in intra-universe dynamics. He was forced to take retirement because he was showing signs of dementia and simply couldn't be trusted to process information mentally, let alone communicate what he knew or thought to others.

Chapter Nine

Lou decided to examine other motives for the death of Father Dunkel. He wondered about liturgical reasons, so he arranged to interview Mrs. Hoffman, the church secretary, on Monday, November 8.

When Lou arrived, Mrs. Hoffman offered him coffee and a donut. Lou accepted, thankful for the refreshment. It was a long drive from Grand Haven to Mesick, a journey of a couple of hours.

"This is really exciting!" Mrs. Hoffman said, smiling, seemingly full of joy. "I feel like I'm right in the middle of an exciting drama."

"Sorry to disappoint you, Mrs. Hoffman, but while this may be exciting to you, to me it's just a job. Please don't take that wrong, for I like the people I meet and the challenge of solving the crime. But, unlike television, it doesn't all come together nicely. It takes fact-finding, thinking, deductive reasoning, and of course, some luck. So, I'm sorry to disappoint you, but you go ahead and enjoy this. I'll just get as much information as I can and add it to my data base."

"Okay, you'll need my full name and address, right?"

"No, Mrs. Hoffman, 'church secretary' is all I need."

"I see. But you want to know what I saw the morning of the murder."

"We can start there if you wish."

"Actually, I didn't see anything. I wasn't at the church. My family and I were in Whitehall, visiting my parents. We went to Mass at the local Catholic church."

"How about we just stick to a simple interview where I ask the question and you answer it to the best of your ability. Okay?" Lou asked, realizing Mrs. Hoffman wasn't under his control.

"Okay. Do you want more coffee?"

"No, thank you."

"Do you have a dog with you?"

Lou shook his head. "No, my dog stays at home."

"Do you have a side-kick, like Dragnet's Joe Friday? You know, 'Just the facts, ma'am'."

"No sidekicks—I have people who work with me, but they are not colorful or especially appealing to the public. Let's do the interview now, okay, Mrs. Hoffman?"

"Fine. But, do I need an attorney? People who are interviewed on television usually want their attorney with them. How about me? Do I need a lawyer?"

"No." Lou spoke slowly, trying to calm her. "To begin, I just need some basic information about Father Dunkel."

"A fine man, a bit pushy, not easy to work with, but in the eyes of our members he is a wonderful priest."

"Let's stay with that thought. How would you best describe him?"

"I just did. Fine man, pushy, difficult to work with, and loved by his parishioners. You want more?"

"Tell me about his personality—how he got along with his parishioners. Did he have any enemies? Things like that."

"Heaven's no."

Lou was getting nowhere. "May I talk to your church maintenance man?"

"You can if you want. Mr. Sheehy won't be much help. He doesn't talk much. He just does his work, keeps to a schedule, works hard."

"I'd like to talk to him."

"This is his day off."

"Does he live around here?"

"I can't give you confidential information. It's our policy."

"Will he be here tomorrow?" Lou asked.

"Yes. We have a funeral in the morning, followed by a luncheon, so Mr. Sheehy must be on hand."

"I'll stop by and chat with him tomorrow then."

"I'll look at his appointment book and see if he has time for you."

"Your maintenance man has an appointment book?" Lou asked hesitantly.

"Ours does."

"Who would make an appointment to see him?"

"Nobody yet, but we can't have people just stopping in expecting Mr. Sheehy to stop on a dime and converse with them. He's a busy man."

"So, if I were a salesman of janitorial supplies, I'd need an appointment to see Mr. Sheehy?"

"Of course. That is, if you want his undivided attention."

"I guess I'll be on my way, Mrs. Hoffman."

"But, we didn't have our interview yet."

"I got the facts, ma'am. I have what I need. Thank you for the coffee and donut."

"Okay, would you like a biscuit for your dog? Colombo would take a biscuit for his dog."

"Of course, I'll take a biscuit for Sam. She loves treats."

"I don't think I helped you learn much about Father Dunkel," admitted Mrs. Hoffman.

"Oh yes, you did." Lou glanced at his notes and said, "You told me he is a fine man, pushy, difficult to work with, and loved by parishioners. Where else would I learn this?"

"Oh, good. Glad I could help. You have a nice day."

The next morning, November 8, Lou went back to Mesick hoping to see Mr. Sheehy. As he pulled up to the church, he saw a man walking between the church and school carrying a snow shovel. A dusting of snow was expected around noon. "Lash Sheehy? May I have a word with you?" Lou asked loud enough to be heard a half-block away.

"Do you have an appointment?" Lash replied with a chuckle.

"Do I need one?" Lou asked, hardly believing what he just heard.

"Of course not. Mrs. Hoffman told me about your visit yesterday, and I couldn't pass up a chance for a little fun."

"I'm Lou Searing, investigating the murder of Father Dunkel and I have a few general questions." They shook hands.

"We're having a funeral here in a couple of hours. Walk with me to the school. I need to open some doors for the women putting on the luncheon."

After the doors were opened, Lash invited Lou to have a seat in the cafeteria.

"I think I can give you what you need. Father Dunkel was quite a study in human nature."

"Mrs. Hoffman was of little help."

"Mrs. Hoffman is a wonderful, caring, and effective secretary. Father hired her after her husband died. She gets the bulletin out, she's great at handling Father's calendar. In other words, she's a perfect secretary, at least perfect as far as our little parish goes."

"Okay, let's get this going," Lou began. "Tell me about Father Dunkel."

"Complex man. I've known him for a few years and I've yet to understand him. He was hot-headed. He wasn't a people-person. Forgive me for saying so, but to my way of thinking, he was an ineffective parish priest. We've lost members and we haven't seen a new member in three or four years. People here were afraid that if they complained, the bishop would close the parish, and this would devastate a loyal following."

"Were there skeletons in his closet?"

"He had a couple, if you ask me. The first was his inability to listen. That may not be a skeleton, but it was a problem for the parish. When you don't listen, you distance yourself from others, and Father was very good at this. He always seemed to carry a chip on his shoulder. He needed to be right. There was no room for compromise."

"And yet, I hear people say he was so loved."

"Go figure."

"Did he have enemies among his parishioners, someone who could have shot him because of an unresolved issue between the two?" Lou asked.

"A few people could have shot Father Dunkel, but nobody would. There's some tension in the parish, but murder? Nobody would go that far, nobody!"

"Thanks, Lash. You've been quite helpful."

Lou was at home collecting wood for a fire on the beach at the twilight of November 10. Beach chairs, the makings for s'mores, and a warm fire were ready as darkness engulfed the Lake Michigan shore. This was normally a summer activity, but the temperatures had been on the mild side of late, so Lou decided to get in one more beach fire before the end of the season.

Several neighbors would wander over, as everyone was welcome. The Searings' son, Scott, and his family would come if they could. A beach fire was a time to let stress and anxiety bury themselves in the sand. This was as close to heaven as one could get, living on the shore of Lake Michigan.

Just after the fire was lit and people began to appear with beach chairs and sweaters, Lou's cell phone rang.

"Mr. Searing?"

"Yes. Who's calling?"

"We're the sisters you see at the Chesaning Craft Show. This is Linda."

"Sisters as in nuns?" Lou asked, not remembering sisters in particular at the craft shows. He'd sold his mysteries there, written versions of murders he had solved over the past 16 years.

"Not Catholic sisters. We're the Wille sisters—Carol, Linda, and Beth. We wear sweatshirts with the word 'Sisters' on them."

"Oh, yes, of course. Now that I've placed you, how can I help you?"

"Do you have a few minutes?"

"Actually, this isn't the best time, but I want to hear what you have to say. Carol and I are hosting our last beach party."

"Oh, I'll call again at a better time."

"No, go ahead. I want to hear what you have to say."

"I'll make it short."

"Fine. Go ahead."

"The three of us were in St. Joseph's the day Father Dunkel was murdered. We were seated where we always sit, left side, second pew. I'm pretty sure I saw the man who shot Father. I didn't see him shoot him, but I, and my sisters as well, recall seeing a stranger in that first pew. Not only was he a stranger but other things caused me to look at him on and off. He was dressed up, which is not common in our church. He was alone, which again is a bit odd; most men are with family or wives or friends. But the most interesting thing is that, when I saw his profile, it was like I was looking at George Washington. I even whispered to my sister, 'Whose profile is that, the man in the suit in the front pew?' She didn't hesitate, but whispered back 'George Washington.' He didn't have on a wig, and if I'd seen him full face, I imagine he wouldn't bear any resemblance to George. But it was uncanny. I'm sure that if I saw him in a lineup, from the side, I could identify him."

"This is great news, and I thank you very much."

"We really don't want to get involved, but we have such respect for you and your work that we had to tell you."

"I'm glad you did! Your phone number is now in my cell phone data base. I'll call if I need to discuss this further. Thanks for calling, Linda."

"Enjoy your beach party, Lou."

The neighbor who lived north of the Searings, Jake Gomez asked Lou point blank, "What famous singer will you invite to your beach party next summer?"

Jake was referring to the visit by Neil Diamond last summer at the Searing's annual beach party. What is the story behind the story? Did you go to high school with him?"

"No, nothing like that. Several years ago, before he traveled in his private jet the two of us were grounded in Chicago due to a snowstorm that closed O'Hare.

"He had a concert at Western Michigan University in Kalamazoo that night. I told him I was going to rent a car and head home. I offered to take him to Kalamazoo. The trip was several hours of slipping and sliding. Dozens of cars were in the median between New Buffalo and Kalamazoo.

"Anyway, I got him to Kalamazoo in time for his concert. Read Field house was filled to capacity in spite of the inclement weather. As he was taking his belongings from the car he told me if he could ever help me to call him. He gave me his card."

"So, you cashed in."

"Everyone seemed to enjoy seeing him and listening to his hits."

"Oh, Lou, you and Carol gave your guests an evening to remember. Who will be our entertainer next summer?" Jake asked.

"Carol is trying to arrange a visit by the magician, Copperfield. I do believe he could make Lake Michigan disappear."

"Would that be cool?"

"It's a long shot, that's for sure."

Jack Kelly called to say he had found further information on Tyrone Babcock. "I'll share with you now if you have a few minutes?"

"For you, I always have a minute."

"Tyrone, known as Ty, was a good kid. He was raised in a Catholic home, and he had no siblings. He was an altar boy, groomed for the priesthood, but he excelled in physics and decided to be a scientist. He was valedictorian of his high school class. He got bachelor's and master's degrees from Loyola University and then to Notre Dame.

"I don't know what happened to him after Notre Dame. Perhaps he married? I don't know why he was interested in physics or what happened to him while he was earning his bachelor of science and his master's degrees. His life during that time would give us a more thorough picture of the man. I'll keep working."

Chapter Ten

On Thursday, December 10, Lou chose to talk to Mark Miller. He contacted Mark's lawyer, Lora Clements, introduced himself, and explained his purpose. Lora felt a meeting would help her client.

Arrangements were made for the three to meet in a Wexford County jail interrogation room. Lora waited with her client. Lou introduced himself to Mark, stating that he had a few questions.

"Ask me anything you want. I've nothing to hide."

"All right. Where were you Sunday morning, October 30 at the 9:00 Mass?"

"I was out of town. I went to the University of Michigan football game on Saturday. I stayed in a motel, slept in, and drove home in the morning, getting there about eleven, I think."

"Were you with anyone at the game?"

"No, I went alone."

"Do you have a ticket stub or a program?"

"No, I put both in the wastebasket at the motel."

"Which motel?"

"Comfort Inn in Ypsilanti."

"Did you keep a receipt from the motel?"

"No. I stopped at a rest area on the way home and emptied my pockets. I had no need for it."

"Did anyone see you at the U of M game?"

"I didn't see anyone I knew. It may seem odd, but not one of the one hundred and ten thousand was familiar to me."

"How about the person who sat next to you in the stadium? Can you identify him or her?"

"I never really looked at him. We talked during the game, but I never looked him in the eye. He had been drinking, as I recall, and he probably wouldn't be able to pick me out of a line-up."

"If we contacted the ticket office and asked about your ticket, I assume they could verify that you were in the stadium?" Lou asked.

"I don't think so. I bought the ticket from someone I didn't know the day before. He asked if I wanted a good deal on a ticket. I said 'sure', and paid him for the ticket."

"Did you register in your name at the Comfort Inn?"

"Yes."

"So, they should have evidence that you checked in there."

"Yes, they should."

"The next day you drove home?"

"Yes."

"Did you stop anywhere along the way?"

"No comment."

"No comment?" Lou asked, surprised. "Did you stop for breakfast? Stop to see a friend? Go to church somewhere?"

"No comment."

"Okay, enough games. Were you in St. Joseph's Catholic church the morning of October 30th?"

After a telling pause, once again Mark said, "No comment."

Lou sighed. "I'm not telling you what to say, for I only want the truth. If you don't deny being in that church, your attorney is going to have a difficult time convincing a judge and jury that you are innocent of murder."

Mark didn't say a word.

"The main point of contention is your whereabouts from the time you checked out of the Comfort Inn until noon."

"I'm not going to say."

"That's your right, Mark. Whatever it is you don't want to share may be none of my business. But, I can assure you that you need an alibi, a witness, someone to vouch for you if you weren't in St. Joe's Sunday morning because we have a witness who says you were."

"I hear you, but I have nothing to say."

"Do you recall where you were Sunday morning?"

"Yes."

"But you don't want to share because where you were is embarrassing. Or, does it perhaps give reason to suspect you of some other crime?"

"No comment. But, I didn't kill that priest."

"That's all for now. I may be back to ask more questions."

Lou talked briefly to Lora outside the interrogation room. "Go ahead and cite attorney/client privilege, but do you know where he was the morning of the murder?"

"No, I don't," Lora admitted. "He won't tell me, either."

"He's hiding something he doesn't want known."

"There is a security video showing Mark entering the motel office in Ypsilanti," Lora began. "He appeared to pay for his room and then walked out the door, entered his car and drove away. There was no one in the car."

"Thanks. I have a gut feeling that this man is innocent. But, if he doesn't cooperate, you're going to have a tough row to hoe."

"I know."

On Friday, November 11, Bishop Grether called Lou asking him to visit. Lou drove to Cadillac and entered the Diocese offices. The receptionist said, "Mr. Searing, Bishop Grether is expecting you. Go right in."

"Thank you."

Lou opened the door to a spacious, yet simple, office. The walls were covered with photos representing the parishes in the Diocese. There were also photos of the bishop with Pope Francis and other Vatican dignitaries. The bishop invited Lou to sit in a soft leather chair in front of a coffee table. Cups of coffee and cookies were brought in.

'This must be quite important for you to request my presence," Lou began.

"You're the most significant person in this sad and complicated drama."

"I don't know about that, necessarily. I'm just trying to piece the whole thing together, to figure out why Father Dunkel died and who killed him."

"Yes, I know, but you're being called to a greater task."

"I am?" Lou said astonished.

"I need your help outside of the murder."

"I'll help if I can. What do you need?"

"This is not the first time one of my priests has been threatened. In fact, it's the third threat, but the first time the crime was actually carried out."

"<u>Three</u> attempted murders?" Lou was dumbfounded.

The bishop shook his head sadly. "The first threat came to one of our larger parishes. The senior priest was threatened and warned to stay more or less in hiding. Apparently some of his recent homilies bothered someone or a group."

"Did he stay out of the public eye?"

"I demanded he not celebrate Mass until I felt comfortable having him do so. The second threat occurred in a town along Lake Michigan. This priest was informed that he would be locked in a confessional and gassed."

"What was his perceived transgression?"

"A confessor had shared something with the priest, who had responded that he would need to contact the legal and mental health authorities. The confessor was under the impression that the priest could say nothing outside of the confessional, and the confessor became agitated to the point that he threatened to kill the priest if word got out about his transgression."

"Being a priest can be a very dangerous job," Lou said.

"Oh, Mr. Searing, you don't know the half of it. Working with people, all kinds of people, is very challenging. Anyway, in the murder of Father Dunkel, a threat was obviously carried out."

"I sense there's another threat, and that's why you want to talk to me?"

"Yes."

"Who is threatened this time?"

"Me."

"Who's upset with you?"

"Lots of people; priests, members of the church, community leaders, the list goes on and on."

"But, who wants you dead?"

"I don't know. I just know that the threat is real, and I'm scared."

"Can you tell me what you know?"

"That is one of the conditions. If I talk to anyone about this, the end of my life is imminent."

"So, I didn't hear anything today?"

"That's right. But come with me to the window on the east side of my office. Stay back a bit so nobody will see you, but I believe high-powered telescopes are aimed at my office. Look out on the street, and you'll see a SUV—looks like a Jeep. See it?"

"Yes."

"I assure you that whoever is in that vehicle is following you. When you leave, you'll note that the vehicle will follow you."

"Starting right now?"

"No, you probably haven't realized it, but I imagine you've been tracked for at least a few days. I took the risk of having you come up here knowing they would suspect I talked to you. After all, you are about as famous a detective as this state has seen."

"You think this vehicle is associated with whoever killed Father Dunkel and threatened the other two priests?"

"Yes."

"Do you know who they are, or why the threats?"

"No."

"Have you talked to the police, so they can track this vehicle?"

"No, I haven't gone to the police. I'm telling you because I believe you can solve this before I or anyone else is harmed."

"Talk about pressure, Bishop!" Lou said, smiling nervously.

"It's <u>your</u> gift from God. I'm only asking you to apply that gift to the threats against His church."

"I guess I'm honored by your trust, but I think this is a lot bigger than me. In fact, I know it is."

"I believe in you, Mr. Searing, and I believe God will work through you."

"Well, first of all, please get on your knees and pray that I'll be guided by the Holy Spirit and my guardian angel. I'll need all the help I can get."

"Bless you, Mr. Searing."

"Thank you." Lou walked from the office, took the stairs to the first floor, walked out of the building and got into his car.

Chapter Eleven

Nobody followed him on the drive to Grand Haven. His mind seemed to wander and he wanted to talk to his friend, Jack.

"These are crazy times."

"What makes you say that?" Jack asked.

"I'm not one of those longing for the good old days, but I wonder whatever happened to peaceful communities, friendly neighbors, kids watching the Mickey Mouse Club on TV. Now you can't let a kid out of your sight because whoever looks at him or her could be a pedophile. Kids are glued to iPhones and video games. Families don't even eat together—everyone is on the go. I guess I long for the good old days every once in a while."

"But the good old days weren't necessarily good," Jack reminded Lou.

"Oh, I know that. I'm a realist. I know we've evolved in many ways, but the human psychic is still sensitive to others. Most people know that love is still the most amazing force in the world."

"You bring this up after meeting with the bishop," Jack said, recalling Lou's calendar. "That tells me the reverend either longs for the good old days or is in the middle of some crisis."

"You got that right. The answer is, the middle of a crisis and the rough part is he expects me to solve it. People get the misperception that since I've solved so many murders, I can stop a bullet with one hand and jump over tall buildings. Well, I can't. I'm just as helpless as the next person."

"What does he want you to handle, if it's any of my business?"

"Of course it's your business. You'll probably be the one to break the case. I just go along for the ride. After all, a coach is only as good as his team, and that goes for investigating crime."

"Bring me on board then. Let me start thinking about it."

"Keep this between you and me. I sense the bishop told me things that he would not want leaked."

"My lips are sealed as they always are. You know that, Lou."

"The bishop reports that priests in the Northwest Michigan Diocese are being threatened. Our murder is the third threat, but the only one that succeeded. Now the bishop himself has been threatened. He's certain my car is being watched and that when I left his office I would be followed. To the best of my knowledge, I'm not being followed."

"So, you need to find who is making these threats against priests and now against the bishop."

"That's right," Lou replied. "And with no staff, no resources, no clues, and no suspects."

"Where do we start, Lou?"

"I think we contact the U.S. Conference of Bishops and see if they know of any threats against priests."

"I'll do that."

"Then I see a think-tank at our home where at least five of the team brainstorm."

"Who are the five?" Jack asked.

"I'm thinking Maggie, Belle, you, and me."

"That's four."

"I know, but there will be others. Maybe Carol, maybe our son, Scott, from Grand Rapids. Maybe one of our grandsons. Who knows who will show up—the more brain power the better."

Monday, November 13, Jack inquired of the Conference of Bishops if they were aware of threats or murders of priests. The head of the conference said he knew of nothing. From time to time threats are made around major issues, but at the moment, it was pretty quiet.

Lou invited people to a think-tank party. Maggie, who helped him with the first six cases, was able to make it. Belle, who acted as detective in <u>Death in the Choir Loft</u>, would hand the baton to her lead tenor and come to Grand Haven from Chelsea. Jack Kelly could make it, of course. Scott Searing couldn't make it, but Lou's grandson, Jackson, would drive over from Grand Rapids.

So, the party was a "go" a mere 48 hours after Lou envisioned it. As people arrived, they were introduced to one another. The only one unknown to the others was Jackson, who was welcomed into this group of brains and successful crime-solvers.

"Sort of out of my league," Jackson told Lou.

"Don't hold back, Jackson," Maggie said. "When your grandpa has a think-tank party, there's nothing but ideas and 'what ifs'. We have a good time. The more an idea is discussed, the easier it is to adopt it as plausible or to drop it as not viable."

The event would be held in Lou and Carol's den. Wood was brought in and piled near the fireplace. An oval dining room table was carried in for people to sit around and write on if they wished.

Carol prepared a veggie tray with a variety of dips. She also provided an ice bucket and a tray of glasses. Lou brought drinks into the den for people to enjoy.

As soon as everyone arrived, Lou opened the session by saying, "This evening is dedicated to our brains and our experience and all we know about solving a murder. This is going to be a free-flow of ideas, theories, and possible motives and antagonists. I'll set the stage, and then we'll just move into free expression of whatever comes to mind. I'll take some notes in the event that we strike gold with an idea that needs follow-up.

"Is everyone ready?" Lou asked. Everyone nodded in the affirmative.

Lou began. "The bishop of the Diocese of Northwest Michigan reports to me in confidence that there have been threats to priests in his diocese, and more recently to him personally. One of the threats led to murder—Jack and I are working to solve that one now. The bishop has no idea who could be threatening them or what or where the next confrontation will be, but he certainly hopes that wherever it is, no one will be injured or killed.

"Our mission this evening is to try to shed some light on this situation: who, why, et cetera. After a few minutes of thinking, someone can start a free-flow of ideas."

It was silent except for the crackling fire casting a glow and warming everyone. After about five minutes seventeen-year-old Jackson spoke up.

"Since I was encouraged to participate, I'll begin by saying it seems to me we're dealing with anger or revenge on behalf of some group. I think it would take more than one person to strike terror in the bishop's mind. So, I think a group of some kind feels threatened, or unhappy or downright angry and wants to get back at the church, specifically priests and the bishop."

"I agree," Belle offered. "I don't see how any of us can know what's going on in the mind of someone wanting to harm priests. I think we need to concentrate on how the criminals will carry out their threats. Once they're apprehended, a motive may be uncovered."

"I see your point, but I do think we can work on motive," Jack Kelly said. "It would help to know if the threat originates with pro-lifers protesting at abortion clinics within the diocese. Or, it may come from those who don't think the church is moving fast enough to give women a greater role in the church. I just think if we knew what is causing the anger, wish for revenge, or need to strike at the church, it would help us get to the perps."

Jackson offered another thought. "I've been trying to think of what these terrorists could do to cause the greatest fear and to harm people, if not kill them. The more I think about it, I think they would be the most successful by using the body and blood of Christ to inflict their pain."

"What does that mean?" asked Belle, who was Protestant.

Jack Kelly answered for young Jackson. "It means that poisoning the wine consumed by the priest and many of the members of the congregation would strike fear into people. Once someone got sick from partaking of the wine, or if an occasional host was poisoned, it would stop people from receiving Jesus, which is the point of the Mass. All I'm saying is, if I were to get into the minds of the enemy, poisoning the host would cripple the church."

Lou interjected. "Thanks, Jack and all of you for good thoughts. Let's take a short break. Good thinking!"

For several minutes, folks helped themselves to fudge and talked about Lou and Carol's beautiful home and cozy den. Then Lou brought everyone back to the task at hand.

"Does anyone have a thought or something to add to what we've heard before the break?"

Maggie, who had been quiet most of the time, spoke up. "I think this is the work of amateurs. I think it's a local group who haven't any idea how to pull off a major crime. I don't think Father Dunkel's murder can be attributed to whoever wants to strike fear into the bishop and other priests. So, as far as I can see, the murder is a separate issue."

"I think Maggie is right," Jack Kelly replied. "If this were the work of some nationwide conspiracy, it would be easy to uncover. The bishop would not know of it. They would attack under a veil of secrecy."

"Excuse me for interrupting," Lou said, "but, why is the diocese of Northwest Michigan being targeted? If you really wanted to make a statement, you'd concentrate on Detroit, and the archbishop."

Jack replied, "It has to be some local initiative. A local group or person is angry, choosing to strike back."

Belle added, "Which brings us back to why someone is angry and wants revenge? Perhaps we need to look toward Right to Life, Voice of the Faithful, a parish perhaps expecting to be closed, or just a sick wacko who can't comprehend the implications of his actions."

Belle then said, "If we look at an individual, the reasons narrow to what would infuriate a person or a couple. I'm thinking of a marriage annulment that is taking forever, or was denied. Or, a kid not being accepted into a seminary. Or, a couple not allowed to be married in the church. Or, perhaps a fiery exchange between a choir director and a priest or a member over some conflict."

Lou countered, "I doubt this is coming from an individual or couple. People angry at the church, or a decision of a religious authority, or behavior of a religious person generally just leave the parish. They take an "I give up," attitude and move on to another parish, or church, or religion. I mean, what could anger someone so much that they are willing to risk prison time forever for a cause?"

Jackson, who had wandered into the living room to sit quietly in grandpa's leather chair, returned, waited so as not to interrupt someone, and added, "I think we may be missing the obvious by looking for a motivation within the church. My guess is that we'll find the murderer killed Father Dunkel for a reason outside of church doctrine. The fact that he's a priest brings attention to the church, but maybe we should think outside of that box. As ridiculous as it sounds, Father could have cut off someone on the highway, and the guy became consumed by road-rage and decided to make Father pay for his error."

"Good point, Jackson," Lou replied. "Let's stay with that idea for a minute. If he is right, the suspect pool would become thousands. Unless Father mentioned such an encounter to someone willing to share, we'll never understand that motivation."

Maggie added, "That's true, but what Jackson has done is to force us to think outside of the church. Thank you, Jackson!"

Lou responded, "I like all of your ideas. I encourage you to sleep on what we've heard and discussed. Other ideas will come to you."

There was silence once again. If one could see mental energy, he would have seen an aura hovering over the think-tank group. "Let's take Lou's lead and call it a night," Belle suggested, sensing it was time to break from thinking.

Lou announced, "Maggie and Belle are staying with us tonight. Jackson and Jack, you're welcome to bed down here as well."

"Thanks, Lou, but I'm going home," Jack Kelly said.

"I'll take you up on your invitation, Grandpa. I'm tired from this exciting evening."

"Good. When you awake, the aroma of bacon in the frying pan and waffles on the griddle might spark a new idea that makes sense. Not that everything shared this evening doesn't. All thought is good and helpful."

"Thanks, Lou, for hosting this get-together," Belle said. "We're making progress, if only in coming up with various scenarios."

"Thank you all for your thoughts. I know I don't have to say this, but I'm going to. What was said and heard in this home this evening stays in this home. Understood?" Four heads nodded.

Chapter Twelve

A few people demonstrated outside of the Wexford County Courthouse where the prosecutor's office was located. People carried signs, "Justice for Mark Miller! You've got the wrong man!" and, "It's Miller Time—Free HIM!"

One also held a sign that read, "Honk if Miller is Not Guilty" which seemed to elicit blaring of horns all day long. Police asked the protestors to remove that sign, but they refused citing the First Amendment.

Mark's neighbor and good friend, Victor Majors, went to the Wexford County Jail every day to see Mark. "I've gathered a few people who are praying for you. In fact, they've started a prayer chain, and now more than a hundred people are thinking of you and praying for you every day."

"That's comforting. Thank you," Mark responded.

"We've also started a defense fund to help you with expenses once your case goes to court. A friend who's an award-winning defense lawyer in the Traverse City area has agreed to assist in your defense for no fee."

"You did this for me?"

"It's the least I can do," Vic replied. "You're a good man, and you don't deserve this injustice. People want to help. I'm just a means to that end. I don't know if you've heard, but protestors are picketing outside the county courthouse, carrying placards proclaiming your innocence."

"You did all of this for me?" Mark asked again. He'd been unaware that Vic was stepping up on his behalf.

"I'll be back tomorrow to pray with you. I know you're innocent, and I'll offer whatever support is necessary to secure your freedom."

"Thank you, Victor. I appreciate all you're doing. Thank you so much."

When Lou contacted the alumni office at Notre Dame, asking to speak to someone who could locate some former students and faculty, he was transferred to Karen Trapp.

"I'm trying to locate a Dr. Winslow who's a professor emeritus in your physics department," Lou explained.

"One moment please." Lou was on hold for a minute or two.

"Dr. Winslow lives in Chicago. I can't give you his phone number or address because it's confidential."

"I'm a detective from Michigan. I'd like to interview him about a murder in northwest Michigan. I can go through the process of getting a court order, but it'd be much easier if you'd just tell me."

"Okay," Karen relented. "I could be fired, but I'll tell you." She told Lou his phone number. "He lives in Lake Towers in Chicago. The address is 6000 Lake Shore Drive."

"Thank you very much. How about Dr. Nix?"

"He is not an alumnus, but a professor who is on sabbatical. Last I heard, he was at Boston College.

"Okay, can you tell me anything about Tyrone Babcock?"

A minute later he heard, "I don't have any information about him."

"How about a professor named Albert Dunkel."

After a pause, Karen said, "He lives in Mesick, Michigan. He is a priest at St. Joseph's Catholic Church."

"Do you keep records of requests like mine?" Lou asked.

"Yes."

"Has anyone previously requested information about the people I'm asking about?"

"That'll take a little searching. Do you want to wait, or would you like me to call back?"

"I'll hold."

It was quiet for about five minutes until Karen returned, "Are you still there?"

"Yes."

"Good. First of all, I don't have any record of anyone asking about Tyrone Babcock, Dr. Winslow, or Dr. Nix. But, I do show someone asking about Dr. Dunkel."

"Can you tell me who that was?" Lou asked.

"Dr. Winslow, and that was about two months ago."

"Thank you, Karen. You have been most helpful."

Lou called Jack to see if he wanted to go to Chicago. The company would be appreciated. "Normally, I'd go, but Elaine and I have planned a trip to Traverse City and I want to honor that commitment."

So Lou asked Carol, "How about a drive to Chicago tomorrow? Is that something you'd like to do?"

"Why would I want to go to Chicago?" Carol asked.

"Oh, I don't know. A little shopping, a little sightseeing, a meal in a nice restaurant?"

"Get real, Lou. You mean 'a little putting up with your nervousness of driving into Chicago and wanting out as soon as your mission is complete'?"

"Well, yes, I guess you're right."

"No thanks, unless you <u>need</u> me to go with you."

"Nope, just offering you the opportunity."

"Could you fly over and back?" Carol asked. "It's so much faster and convenient."

"You've a point there."

Lou looked for a cheap flight from Ford Airport in Grand Rapids to O'Hare in Chicago. Instead, he found a flight from Muskegon to Midway Airport, from where he could get a cab to Lake Shore Drive. He purchased a round-trip ticket, and the next morning, after a short flight, he relaxed in a cab, heading for the heart of Chicago.

When the cab pulled up to Lake Towers, Lou paid the cabbie, took his valise, walked into the lobby, and pushed the button for "Winslow". When there was no response, he pushed it again. A few seconds later he heard a faint, "Yes?"

"Dr. Winslow?"

"Yeah."

"I'm from Michigan and I'd like to talk to you."

"What are you selling?"

"Nothing. I'm investigating the murder of Dr. Dunkel."

"Murder of whom?"

"Father Albert Dunkel."

"Never heard of him."

"That may be, but I'd like to talk to you for a few minutes. Is that okay with you?"

"I guess so. You'll hear a bell and then you can open the door. I'm in Apartment 444, on the fourth floor."

"Thank you, Doctor," Lou replied. He heard the bell, opened the door, and headed for the elevator.

On the fourth floor, Lou looked right and saw a bald man standing in the hall. "I'm here!" the man called.

Lou approached and introduced himself and was shown into the apartment which resembled a man-cave.

"Looks like you're a Chicago sports fan," Lou said, noting photos of the Bears, Black Hawks and White Sox sport teams. "But you're not a Cubs fan?"

"Nope. I like the Sox, and I go to most of their games. I'd offer you something to drink, but other than a shot of Jack Daniels, I can't help you. I don't have visitors so I'm not prepared to be a host."

"How about a glass of ice water. Do you have that?" Lou asked.

"Oh, sure. Make yourself at home. I'll get it."

Lou made his way around piles of books and magazines on the floor and looked out the window. Before him was a panoramic view of the Lake Michigan waterfront."

"This is a nice view of the Chicago skyline."

"Yeah, if they ever cleaned these windows, I could admire it. But, the landlord isn't interested in clean windows, so I don't make an issue of it."

Dr. Winslow offered Lou a glass of water. "Here you go. What did you say your name was again?"

"Lou Searing."

"Searing, like super-hot?"

"That's right. And your first name, Dr. Winslow?"

"Reggie. My parents named me Reginald, for what reason God only knows. I got beat up as a kid, but I suppose I'd have been beaten up for something else, if not for my name."

"Thank you for meeting with me."

"You're welcome, I guess. Why are you here?"

"I'm a private investigator, working on a murder that took place in northwest Michigan. The victim is someone you know, a former colleague of yours named Albert Dunkel."

"Crazy son-of-a-bitch," Winslow said off-handedly.

"So you know of whom I speak."

"Ruined some lives—a miserable human being."

"That's what I want to learn about."

"You say he was murdered?" Dr. Winslow asked.

"That's right. He was shot during Mass in his church in Mesick, Michigan."

"Why would the Catholic Church ever make him a priest? I know they're hurting for men to become priests, but they mustn't have any standards for priests."

"I don't know about that. I'm just trying to find out who killed him."

"Well, I don't know the answer to that."

"Do you know anyone who might be upset enough with Dunkel to end his life?"

"I was on dissertation committees with him at Notre Dame. If he didn't like a student as a person, or if he didn't personally direct the dissertation, he would find a way to humiliate the candidate, rip apart his or her research, and deny the degree. It was sad. It was wrong. I still almost get sick thinking about it."

"You voted with him?"

"Yeah, I did. I was afraid of what he'd do if I didn't. I needed tenure at the time, and if he had a grudge against me, I'd be denied. I couldn't afford it. I was more of a teaching professor than a researcher. It's harder for us to get tenure because we don't generate grants and federal money. So, my earning tenure would take faculty endorsements and I needed Albert's support. I did get it, but at a terrible price."

"Very sad."

"Yes, it is."

"Which students didn't get their Ph.D. degrees while you were there?"

"I might not get the names right, but I think there was a woman named Cally or something like that."

"Kale?" Lou suggested.

"Yes, she was one candidate, and there were two guys. One had an uncommon name, and the other a common name."

"Was the uncommon name Tyrone?"

"That's it. Tyrone Babcock, I believe."

"And the third?" Lou asked.

"Oh yes, the common name. It'll come to me. My memory isn't what it used to be. Just be quiet, it'll pop into my mind." He thought for a few seconds. "Tim!" Winslow blurted out, "Tim O'Shaughnessy! A good Irish name for Notre Dame. Yeah, he was canned too. Bright kid, hard-working, wanted to do subatomic research. Back then it was ground-breaking science. Today, it's common. The emphasis now is sub-subatomic. I don't even know what they call it."

"Whatever happened to Tim?"

"I don't know. I can't keep up with everyone. Let me think a minute. I think he got a position as an assistant professor at a Midwestern college. Colleges usually don't hire faculty without doctorates, but thankfully, somebody saw a bright future and took a chance on him."

"Maybe you'll come up with the school."

"Oh, I will. What I'm searching for usually comes up—it's like my brain needs a research assistant to run to the files to find what I'm trying to say."

"That's an interesting analogy," Lou said, knowing exactly what Reggie meant.

"Ferris State—right there in your home state."

"Is he there now?" Lou asked.

"Yeah. He's earned a good reputation. Students love him."

"Can you describe him?"

"Tall, bald, and you know, this is going to sound if you look at his profile from the side, you'd swear before you was Thomas Jefferson."

"Really?"

"Really. Not the hairline, but the forehead, the nose, the chin."

"So, if I'm looking at him from the side, I should recognize him, right?"

"You should," Winslow said. Then he brightened and smiled. "If you meet Tim, say hello for me. I always liked him."

"I will. Before I go, can you tell me a little about Tim? Does he have a temper?"

"You mean, do I think he killed Dunkel?" Dr. Winslow asked point-blank. "Yes, probably, and I can't blame him. Dunkel took away his chance for a professorship at a prestigious institution. This kid was brilliant—everything Dunkel wasn't."

"So, you really think Tim could have killed Albert Dunkel?"

"Yes. I hope he didn't, but yes, I think he could have."

Lou thanked Reggie for his time, the ice water, and his cooperation. He left his card and asked to be contacted if Reggie had anything else to share.

Lou walked to the elevator, out onto Lake Shore Drive, hailed a cab, and soon was on his way to Midway Airport and his return flight to Muskegon. As Lou pulled into his drive at 11:30 p.m, about an inch or two of snow had fallen. Lou didn't wake Carol, just kissed her on the forehead and got into bed. It had been a long day.

Chapter Thirteen

The next day, November 16, Lou went to Ferris State University in Big Rapids. At the administration building, he was greeted by the receptionist. "How may I help you?"

"I'm looking for a member of the science faculty by the name of Tim O'Shaughnessy."

"I'll ring his office, but I can't assure you he's there. I think he has office hours tomorrow, but we'll see." She rang his office and he answered.

"A gentleman in the reception area would like to talk to you. Shall I send him up?"

"Is he a student, or who is he?"

"Your name, please?" the receptionist asked. Lou handed her his business card. "His name is Lou Searing, from Grand Haven."

"Send him up."

The receptionist said to Lou, "This is your lucky day—his office is on the second floor, Number 231."

"Thank you."

Lou knocked on the door and heard, "Come in, the door's open."

Lou walked in expecting to see a modern-day Thomas Jefferson or George Washington, but he saw nothing of the sort. Lou stuck out his hand and greeted the professor. "I'm Lou Searing. Thanks for meeting with me."

"I have some time, but not a lot. My lab class meets in an hour."

"I'm an investigator looking into the murder of Albert Dunkel."

"That case has been on the news every day," Tim said, a bit annoyed. "You'd think, after a day or two, something else would grab a reporter's attention."

"I suspect it's because a priest was shot. That's rare and scary with the shot being fired during a Mass."

"You're right. It sells newspapers and that's the name of the game. Anyway, you wanted to talk to me?"

"Yes. I understand that you had a bad experience involving Dr. Dunkel when you were a student at Notre Dame."

"Yeah. I'm pretty much over it now, but he was responsible for a glimpse of hell on earth, that's for sure."

"Does that trigger any anger, or intense feelings of revenge?"

"Certainly! Who wouldn't be upset after spending three years of your life and thousands of dollars working toward a degree?"

"How did you express that anger and feelings of revenge?"

"It may sound odd to you, but I decided it was time to change the Catholic Church. Any organization that would choose the likes of Albert Dunkel as a representative is in need of major reform. So, I set about doing what I could in my little corner of the world to open people's eyes to the atrocities."

"Let me get this straight: you're waging a one-man effort to reform the Church,"

"Right. Someone has to step up!"

"Have you threatened anyone?"

"One or two, yes. I need to wake up the sleeping giant."

"You sound like Don Quixote, heading off to slay windmills. The Church is huge."

"I know that. I plan to change the Church one diocese at a time."

Lou decided Tim needed medical help. He hoped the county's mental health office would give therapy to this disillusioned member of society.

"Did you kill Father Dunkel?" Lou asked.

"I most certainly did not! You think I'm crazy?" Lou didn't answer, in voice or in body language, but he thought, *You bet!*

"Father Dunkel could be your first reform," Lou said as he rose and moved to observe Tim's profile.

"Dunkel was a product of the problem," Tim replied. "He could not be reformed. His personality was established. The people needed to expel that nut from their midst. It looks like that's what happened."

"But, you didn't kill Dunkel?" Lou asked a second time.

"Mr. Searing, how could I possibly reform the Catholic Church at the diocese level sitting in prison? Killing Dunkel would have been diametrically opposed to making any progress in my reform efforts."

"Do you admit to threatening priests, and even the bishop?"

"Yes, I'm guilty of that. That's the first phase, intended to shake up the hierarchy."

Lou could see no resemblance to Thomas Jefferson or George Washington in Tim's profile.

Tim continued unperturbed. "Actually, the murder of Dunkel was an unintended consequence of my plan. People's attention would be awakened by the murder, and their thoughts would be on why this happened. Do you see what I'm getting at?"

"I just find it odd that you would take on the Roman Catholic Church in one diocese, believing that you could change anything, anything at all."

"Others have said the same thing, but when God wants things to change, He can change them."

"Wait a minute, Tim. You think God wants the reform you want?"

"Absolutely! People have created the mess we have, and people have to change! It's my quest to lead this movement."

Lou moved toward the office door. "Tim, thanks for talking with me. I encourage you to get help. Pardon me for saying so, but I think your perception of reality is askew."

"You mean, you think I'm mentally ill?" Tim's face became red. Lou wasn't sure what Tim might do in an agitated state. "You think I'm crazy don't you!" Tim rose and headed for the closet. Lou expected to see a gun. His heart beat faster.

Tim opened the door of the closet, and took out a large cross, and held it up facing Lou as if warding off an evil spirit.

"Get out, Satan!" Tim seemed to be in a catatonic state, not conscious of the real world.

"I'll go, Tim. Thanks for talking with me. I'll see myself out. Good luck to you."

Suddenly Tim lowered the cross, his face drenched in sweat. He put the cross down on his desk and sat in his chair. Lou left the office, closed the door, and headed for the front door.

Outside, he sat on a bench in a park and watched students passing from one class to another. He looked at the flower beds and admired the beauty of nature. Soon his thoughts returned to Tim. It saddened him to see a mind so disoriented. Lou wished to change some things in the Catholic Church and others in society in general, but he knew that both society and the Catholic Church were much larger than he was. Some people work all their lives to reform, but they do it with organizations, strategy, and huge budgets.

Lou was quite certain Tim had not killed Albert. Dunkel had been just one of a host of windmills for Tim. Planning a murder and getting away with it could not be done by someone in Tim's mental state.

Lou called Paul Wright, the Dean of the Science Department at Ferris State. "I've just come from a meeting with Mr. O'Shaughnessy and I'm concerned."

"A student-aide was working at the reception desk when you arrived, so your call was not forwarded to me. Tim is no longer a member of our faculty. We love the man. He has provided excellent teaching to our students, but his mental health has deteriorated."

Lou was confused. "But he has an office."

"Yes. We allow him his office. It's a place where he feels safe. We're convinced he isn't a threat to anyone. To remove him from his office would be cruel, and we can't bring ourselves to destroy him, for he's been through so much. He's happy and quiet most of the time in this sanctuary. As they say, we're letting well enough alone."

"I understand. I wanted to meet him, because I'm investigating the murder of Father Dunkel, and I thought Tim might have had a role in it."

"Mr. Searing, I assure you that Tim should not be considered a suspect. I'm his legal guardian, and he hasn't been out of his office or my home for two years."

"Two years?"

"That's right. He has become like my son."

"He talked about his mission to reform the Catholic Church."

"Pure fantasy. It's all in his sick mind."

"Do you know of a relationship, if any, with Father Albert Dunkel?"

"That man is evil, and we do not discuss evil."

"Did he harbor hatred toward Fr. Dunkel for what he did when Tim was at Notre Dame?"

"We do not discuss the man."

"I see."

Lou pulled into his driveway south of Grand Haven, greeted Carol with a hug and a kiss, and patted their golden retriever on the head. He noted that Sami their cat couldn't be bothered with any type of greeting, except to sit by her empty bowl, as if to say, "So, you're back, big deal. Now, can I please have some food!"

"How was your trip to Chicago?" Carol asked.

"Let's take a walk and I'll bring you up to date."

"I'm ready."

Wearing reflective vests for safety, they walked north along the road in front of their home. Lou explained all he had experienced and learned in Chicago and this morning at Ferris State.

"Crazy is all I'll say," Carol replied. "Does any of your research make sense to you?"

"Yes, and no. I can understand what happened, but at the same time, it seems like a made-up fantasy story. I have no choice but to accept it as real, I suppose."

"But, are you any closer to solving the murder?" Carol asked.

"Not really. I've gone from thinking of Tim as suspect number one to thinking I don't have a main suspect."

"You thought Father Dunkel was killed by one of the Ph.D.

students he failed at Notre Dame," Carol remarked. "Is that still your theory?"

"I don't know what to think now."

"Guess we'd better turn around and head home," Carol said.

"Looks like a storm out over the lake. I like walking in the rain, but I suppose we'd better get inside while we're dry."

Mark Miller remained in jail, denied bail. Lou and Lora Clements were frustrated that Mark wouldn't account for his activity Sunday morning, at least in a manner that would demonstrate he wasn't a suspect.

"You won't tell me where you were?" Lora asked.

"No, I won't."

"You realize I can't defend you unless you're honest with me and provide details."

"I understand, but I can't discuss it."

"Well, you're baffling. In the first place, I remain curious, and secondly, as long as you won't explain your whereabouts, you're practically admitting that you shot the priest."

"That's the chance I take."

"I understand."

"Okay, if you change your mind, please let me know. I'll prepare a defense and do what I can to get you out of here."

"Thank you. I appreciate your efforts."

Jack called Lou. "I've got some news for you, my friend."

"I can always use news," Lou replied. "What have you got?"

"I kept wondering why Mark Miller is a suspect, since he has no connection to Notre Dame or to Father Dunkel's past. But, I found out that he and Fr. Dunkel are in the same golf league."

"Interesting connection."

"A lot can happen on and off a golf course that could lead to murder."

"That's it?" Lou asked. "They are in the same league. You have nothing beyond that? No conflict? No arguments? No threats? No cheating?"

"Nope, just information for your case file. You might find something that will tie into golf."

"Okay. As always, thanks, Jack!"

Chapter Fourteen

L ou drove to St. Joseph's Church in Mesick. He had yet to take a good look at the sanctuary thinking the detectives would do a thorough crime scene analysis.

Lou relaxed in the pew where the shooter allegedly sat. He studied the background behind the altar. He imagined the scene, "seeing" Father approach the altar and begin the Mass. Then he looked over his shoulder toward the balcony. He imagined the shooter being up in that balcony with no choir, no cry room, no overflow crowd. No one would see him there, and with a silencer's small "pop" it wouldn't sound like a rifle shot. *Maybe the shot was fired from up there and not from the first pew,* he thought. *But, why would the bald, and well-dressed gentleman accused of the crime sit front and center in the church where he could be seen or photographed?* It made no sense.

Lou silently admonished himself for assuming that the man in the front pew had shot the priest. Maybe it didn't happen that way. He thought he had learned not to assume through other investigations, but apparently he hadn't.

As Lou approached his car to begin the drive back to Grand Haven, his cell phone rang. The caller introduced himself as Del Willingham.

"Yes, Mr. Willingham. How can I help you?"

"I called because I talked with Father Dunkel before he was murdered, and he said something I think you should know."

"I'm listening."

"As I recall our conversation, he seemed depressed," Del began. "I didn't think clinically, although he might have been. During our talk he said he had considered staging murder as a means of proving to the bishop that his life was threatened. If that worked, he could be reassigned."

"Did he offer any details?" Lou asked.

"No, he sort of brushed it off after mentioning it, but in light of what has happened, I thought you should know."

"In 'suicide by cop' someone wanting to die puts himself in a situation where an officer would shoot him. Since you knew Father Dunkel well and since he confided in you, do you think he arranged for someone to shoot him and make it look like suicide?"

"No, I don't think so," Del replied. "He wouldn't do this because of the children. To have children see an attempted murder, either staged or real, just wasn't him."

"Thank you, Mr. Willingham. I appreciate your call."

"Sure. I hope you catch whoever did this."

"I'll try to see justice done."

Lou wanted another talk with Mark Miller, so he called Lora Clements and arranged a meeting for mid-afternoon of that day. In a small, bare conference room, he declined an offer of coffee. Lora accompanied Mark who wore an orange jail-issued jump suit. His hands were cuffed, and after he sat down, his ankles were bound to the chair legs.

"Mr. Miller, thanks for meeting with me once again."

"More questions, huh?"

"Yes, if you don't mind."

"Go ahead."

"Were you in St. Joseph's Catholic Church in Mesick, Michigan, the morning of Sunday, October 30?"

"As I told you last time, I will not say."

"If I may comment," attorney Clements interrupted.

"No, please," Lou said. "I don't want any interruptions."

"Okay. Sorry."

"Nothing to be sorry about. When I interview someone I'm only interested in what they have to say. When I'm finished, I'd be happy to listen to you. If you wish to counsel your client, that's another thing. Okay?"

Lora nodded once. Lou directed his attention to Mark. "It's your right to remain silent about where you were the morning of October 30. But refusing to answer that question won't help me solve this murder. No doubt you have reasons for not disclosing this information. I have no recourse but to think wherever you were is embarrassing or illegal. But, whatever you tell me in this setting either with your attorney present or to me alone, is like talking to a priest. What I hear stays between my ears, in my brain, and I'll keep the confidence. It's important that you understand this. Okay?"

Mark nodded. "I'll tell you, but not my attorney."

"I'll leave," Lora replied. She stood up and walked out of the room.

With only the two men in the room, the interview continued.

"Is this being recorded?" Mark asked.

"No."

"Are we being seen?"

"No."

"Ok, I'll explain where I was that Sunday morning. I'm involved in a ministry in my church. We meet with people and use our faith to help them with real-life issues. To do this work, we have to adhere to very high standards of confidentiality. To state who you meet with, or where, or what the meeting is about, breaks this bond of trust. I absolutely cannot and will not say who I was with or what was being discussed or where I was."

"Thanks for sharing this," Lou replied. "There are ways to share information while maintaining that confidentiality. It happens often. It just isn't common knowledge."

"That matters not. I'd rather go to jail for a crime I didn't commit than give you the information Lora needs to defend me, or, in your case, to take me off the suspect list."

"I understand. Now, at least I can confidently continue the investigation, knowing you're no longer a suspect."

"Whatever you wish to do."

Lou took a deep breath. "Let me ask you this. This person you were meeting—I assume he or she knows you're in jail, and follows media reports, and knows you haven't been forthright in explaining your whereabouts. Isn't it logical that even though you're adhering to confidentiality, that person could, to avoid your possible imprisonment, come forward and explain under oath what you were doing?"

"It's always possible, but I won't ask him or her to do anything."

"I understand. I must say, I admire your moral fiber and your commitment to standards that, if broken, could give you freedom."

Mark simply nodded and hung his head while Lou went to the door to invite attorney Clements back into the room.

Saturday morning, November 19, Lou met with Jack at Paneras Restaurant in Grand Haven. "It's time for a meeting of the minds," Lou announced. "I need your best thinking."

"Lemonade, Lou?"

"No thanks. I just need you to listen and then give me your thoughts."

"Fine with me." Jack settled back in his chair.

"Mark Miller is not a suspect," Lou began. "The fatal shot could have been fired from the balcony in the church, not by the man in the front pew. The man in the pew could be a part of the crime, or he could be a red herring.

"When I look at the three Ph.D. students who were denied the degree at Notre Dame I see this: Ms. Kale is forever angry, but I'm convinced she's not behind the killing. Tyrone Babcock could be involved, but I can't tie anything to him. Tim O'Shaughnessy is mentally ill and likely incapable of killing and I'm convinced he has not been out of the care of his guardian. So, the three who have the most reason to seek revenge don't seem viable suspects."

Lou sighed. "I really haven't researched the people in Dunkel's parish. A few people were angry with him for one reason or another, but there's no evidence that would implicate any of them."

"I think you need a break," Jack suggested.

"You may be right, Jack. I get deep into a case and it just overtakes me. Maybe taking my mind off it will help. Any suggestions?"

"Go to a movie, meditate, play some golf or make a rosary. Any of those should help you come back refocused." Lou had recently begun to learn how to make rosaries. He enjoyed the peace he felt, being alone, and working with his hands instead of his mind.

"Thanks, Jack. I'll take your advice."

After making a rosary to give to a critically ill friend, Lou was ready to get back to work.

He thought, *Maybe I am putting all of my energy into the Notre Dame fiasco. The murder could be totally unrelated to Notre Dame or Dunkel's job before he became a priest.* Lou recalled Jackson's comment and smiled.

On November 21, Lou made an appointment with Father Leonard Adams, a professor at the seminary where Dunkel received his training. Father Adams was Dunkel's spiritual director.

"Thanks for meeting with me, Father."

"The pleasure's mine. How can I help?"

"As you no doubt know, Fr. Dunkel was murdered during Mass in his church on Sunday October 30."

"Yes, the bishop informed us."

"I'm here to ask what you might have to say about this."

"I'm shocked. I'm disturbed. I'm disbelieving. Those were my initial reactions."

"In spite of not believing, can you think of anyone or anything that could be connected to this crime?"

"I honestly can't."

"Father Dunkel received his training here, correct?" Lou asked. Father Adams nodded.

"Did you happen to be on an acceptance committee that chose Albert Dunkel for study at this seminary?"

"I was on the committee."

"Was there any hesitation in accepting him?"

"Every candidate is thoroughly considered. Albert's credentials were excellent in terms of grades, intelligence, ability to hold a job and carry out its responsibilities."

"What about his personality?"

"We received a few letters that addressed his personal skills. We noted that on occasion he could be a bit hot under the collar, but we didn't think it serious enough to prohibit his enrolling."

"How was he as a student?" Lou asked.

"Exceptional. Many instructors were amazed at how much more he knew than they did."

"Did he have the opportunity to study with a priest in a parish?"

"Oh yes, that's part of the training."

"Where and under whom did he study?"

"I'd have to retrieve his file. I can find that now or after the interview, whichever you prefer."

"I'd like it now," Lou replied.

"Not a problem." Father Adams moved to his computer and, in a matter of seconds, said, "He served for six months with Father Kennedy at St. Peter's in Gaylord."

"I'll find his contact information in the diocesan directory," Lou replied. "So, back to Fr. Dunkel. He was a good student here. He passed the judgment of Father Kennedy. And, the bishop assigned him to…?"

"Christ the King, in Petoskey."

"How did he do there?"

"Ah, not so well. It was while he was in Petoskey that we began to see problems."

"What kind of problems?"

"Mostly his immaturity and difficulty dealing with youth in the parish. He wanted to start a class about the early saints, but the kids had no interest in that. They wanted a cause, a way to help the community. They wanted to do what they presumed to be the will of God. Father Dunkel demanded that they study the saints. He even forbade pizza and pop at the youth meetings."

"Goodbye youth," Lou said.

"Exactly. Word eventually got to the pastoral council, who sided with the youth and insisted he be reassigned. The resident priest had no choice but to ask that Father Dunkel be removed from Christ the King."

"Where did he go?"

"He was assigned to a Catholic hospital in Alpena, and there he sort of slid into obscurity. He visited the sick, prayed with them and their families, and served communion. Just when the bishop thought Father Dunkel had found his niche, he refused to give last rites to a woman who had left the church decades before. Apparently she had gotten a divorce, did not get an annulment, and then remarried. Once Father Dunkel heard of this, he insisted she no longer could receive communion, and he refused to offer last rites as her cancer progressed."

"Refusing communion is probably consistent with church doctrine, but refusing to hear her confession and refusing to offer the sacrament of the sick probably is not acceptable."

"The family's complaint went all the way to Rome. Officials in the Vatican supported Father Dunkel, and this further infuriated the family. The woman's son apparently said to Father Dunkel in a fit of anger, "I'll see that you won't have last rites before <u>you</u> die. You will die with sin on your soul. And, if there's a just God, you will rot in hell forever. You are a despicable human being!"

110

"Shortly after this, the bishop brought Fr. Dunkel into the diocese office and gave him an office job. I believe he got counseling at that time as well."

"With this background as a priest, why would the bishop assign him a parish?" Lou asked.

"Supply and demand. The previous priest at St. Joseph's retired. He needed to be replaced as dementia was stealing his mind. The bishop needed to assign a priest or close the parish. He didn't want to close the parish, so he took the chance to put Fr. Dunkel in Mesick. And he asked Fr. Richards to 'keep an eye on him'."

"How long ago was that?"

"Not quite a year."

"Can you give me the name of the family of the hospital patient who was incensed?"

"I really shouldn't without the bishop's permission, but I understand the importance. Again, excuse me while I look at my computer."

A minute later he returned and said, "It's the Holmes family in Grayling. The son's name is Bill. I can give you his home phone."

"Thank you. Will you get in trouble if they ask how I got their name and I tell them?"

"No. In fact, I'll call Bill and talk to him about your investigation. I'll tell him to expect your call."

"Fine. Thank you."

Lou waited an hour or so before calling Bill Holmes.

"Mr. Searing? Father Adams alerted me to your call. How can I help you?"

"I'm investigating the murder of Father Dunkel in Mesick."

"You'll get no tears from me. In fact, I couldn't be happier."

"I'm not calling to measure your joy or pain," Lou began. "I'm simply trying to learn as much about Albert Dunkel as I can. Unfortunately, you had a bad experience with him, and I'm hoping you might shed light on his personality."

"I don't like reliving the hell he put us through, but if you need my help, I'll meet with you."

"Thank you."

Arrangements were made to meet with Bill Holmes and his family. As it turned out, the meeting was only with Bill and it took place in his home. After greetings and refreshments, Bill began. "I guess you're going to ask questions?"

"That's usually the way it works, or perhaps you can tell me about your experience."

"No, I vote for the Q and A."

"Fine. Did you kill Albert Dunkel?" Lou asked bluntly.

"You get right to the point, don't you? No, I did not kill him, at least not physically. I killed him a dozen times in my imagination. I hope that does not make me eligible for jail time."

"Do you know who did kill him?"

"No, but when I find out, I'll give him whatever might make him happy."

"Why did you say, 'him'?" Lou wondered. "Do you know the killer is a man?"

Bill was startled. "No, I assumed."

"Words are like bullets, Mr. Holmes. They can maim with as much accuracy as bullets. By saying 'him', you just cut my suspect pool in half."

"I was using the general pronoun. Of course, I don't know who killed him. How would I know?"

Other than that Bill Holmes was an unhappy man, Lou learned nothing that would help him solve Father Dunkel's murder.

Chapter Fifteen

Fr. Richards of St. Patrick's in Yuma called Lou, offering a suggestion.

"Lou, after every Mass I field questions about finding Father Dunkel's killer and I always have nothing to say. Would you be willing to talk with members who want a briefing? I could record the meeting so others who can't attend could see the tape at their leisure."

"Absolutely! I think that's a great idea. Tell me when and where. If I can make it, I'll be there."

"How about next Wednesday, November 23, at 7:00, in the St. Mary room of the Mesick church? This is very short notice, but with e-mail I'll try to round up a crowd. If people are gone for Thanksgiving, they can view the tape later."

"I can meet with your parishioners on the 23rd. I'd like you to ask people to sign in, and I'd like some video of who's there. Often a person guilty of a crime will attend the funeral or a briefing like you are suggesting."

"I'll arrange for that."

"While I have your attention, I'd like to get your take on something."

"Sure."

"I can't figure out why a church with a popular priest doesn't grow. The man is loved and yet the membership remains stable. You would think the numbers of parishioners would increase. Why is there no growth?"

"I've wondered the same thing. The only thing I can think of is his clinging to the traditional church. People today generally flock to a church with an uplifting ministry, an excellent choir, a viable youth program, and a priest who is personable. Yes, Father Dunkel is loved but he isn't a priest for a modern church."

"Thanks. Your explanation makes sense."

Lou was early for the meeting of sixty-one interested members. Father Richards introduced Lou to the group, noting that they were blessed to have an investigator with his credentials working to solve the crime.

"Thank you, Father Richards. Welcome everyone. Father has told me that many of you ask him for the latest on the investigation, and he's not had any information. I am happy to talk with you. Please realize that I can't give you some facts or names because of confidentiality issues. Nobody wants to jeopardize the investigation.

"I will say that we have uncovered some theories and are seeking evidence. I can also say most assuredly that we're not yet certain who the killer is. If any of you in church the morning of the murder saw anything strange or out of the ordinary, please tell me. I'm available in this group setting, privately, or you may contact me by phone or e-mail. I often receive clues from people who think I know something I don't, or consider what they saw or heard insignificant. Let me decide if it's insignificant."

A high school-aged girl stood to be recognized. Lou invited her to speak.

"I saw a man come into the church with what looked like a rifle case."

"Did anyone else see what… what is your name?" Lou asked.

"Heather Toms."

"Did anyone else see what Heather saw?"

"Yes, I did," said an older woman in the back of the room.

"I can explain that," offered an older gentleman. "I think he's with the company that's putting together our parish directory. I imagine he was carrying a tripod, because I saw a camera bag in his other hand, and he had a camera hanging around his neck."

"Can you describe the man?" Lou asked.

"Ordinary. Nothing about him stood out. He was middle-aged, nicely dressed, full head of hair," Heather replied.

"Did you see where he went after he came into the church?" Lou asked.

"He went up into the balcony."

"Did anyone else see him after he came in?" Lou asked. No one responded.

"This is what I hoped would happen this evening. I realize I'm here to inform you about the investigation, but it's a two-way street. I want to know what you may have seen or heard, either that morning or since."

Many heads in the group nodded, and Lou continued. "As I said, we don't have a viable suspect at the moment. We have talked to several people who knew Father Dunkel before he became a priest and others who knew him as a priest. We've learned that he could show a temper and was easily upset, and in some cases, he infuriated people he encountered as a professor at Notre Dame."

"You mean someone might have killed him because of how they were treated or talked to?" a woman in the front row asked in surprise.

"As you can imagine, people have different temperaments. Some let negative encounters roll off their backs, and others are so offended that they either contemplate doing or saying something quite offensive."

"Okay," Lou paused. "As I said, we're looking at motives. From the autopsy we know he died of a gunshot wound. Forensic measurements taken of the bullet's entrance and exit wounds indicate Father Dunkel was killed with a weapon of a larger caliber than a pistol. The police did find the bullet. It was lodged in the wall next to the tabernacle."

"Did anybody see Father get shot?" a woman near the back asked.

"The only person who thinks she saw the shooter is your organist. She has said she didn't see the gun fire, but she saw a stranger move erratically and leave immediately after Father fell forward. As you no doubt have read in the paper, a Mr. Miller of this community has been arrested and charged with the murder."

"He didn't do nuthin'!" a man shouted.

"Why is he in jail?" another man asked.

"Here's where I must be careful what I say," Lou began. "As I understand it, the person the organist saw resembled Mr. Miller; middle-aged, receding hairline, dressed up. I don't think Mr. Miller was in church. Mr. Miller refuses to explain where he was the morning of October 30. We know where he went the day before and where he spent the night, but we can't account for where he was the morning of October 30."

"That's not enough to lock a guy up!" shouted a man in the audience.

"That's not my doing. I only collect information and hopefully put parts of a puzzle together. I don't work for the prosecutor; what the prosecutors do is their business. For all I know, they have information that's more incriminating."

"I don't mean to be critical of our police, but this sure looks like the work of Barney Fife on the Andy Griffith show," a man in a wheelchair offered. "A lot of bumbling! Mark Miller will be determined innocent. And then, if he has the guts, he'll sue for damaging his reputation and he'll be our community's multimillionaire! And you know who'll pay for this? We will. The taxpayers. This whole thing is ridiculous!"

"You're entitled to your opinion, and I respect that," Lou explained. "Again, I'm only here to give you a briefing."

"So far, everything you've said I've already seen in the paper," said a young woman standing outside of the seating area. "I came here expecting something besides old news." There was a half-hearted round of applause as about a dozen people left the meeting.

Father Richards rose and took the microphone. "I know this is an emotional issue, but I'm embarrassed. Mr. Searing came here from his home in Grand Haven at my request to give you the latest information, and he's doing that. We must respect his need to withhold certain information from us. Please be kind, and think before you speak."

The woman who made the statement about old news spoke again, "I apologize, Mr. Searing. Thank you for coming here to meet with us. We loved Father Dunkel and we were frustrated not to know who took our beloved priest from us."

Lou nodded in accepting her apology. The rest of the meeting was a discussion of how Lou investigates murders, interesting stories from those investigations, and next steps in the Dunkel murder. People lightened up and asked some searching questions about crime-investigation in general. When the briefing was over, Lou received a round of polite applause.

A few people stayed behind to have a private word with Lou. One had even brought a copy of one of his books for an autograph. He obliged her.

Heather stood around waiting for Lou. When he noticed her, he said, "Thank you for your observation. I hadn't heard about a man with a tripod case."

"It wasn't a tripod case, Mr. Searing. It was a rifle case," Heather said with conviction.

"How do you know?"

"Because, I was curious. Just before Mass, I quietly walked up a couple of stairs toward the balcony and cautiously looked for the man. He was leaning over the balcony rail, and he didn't have a tripod. He was positioning a rifle, looking through the scope. I immediately turned and tip-toed downstairs and sat down. I sort of froze. I didn't know what to do so I prayed and watched the drama unfold."

"You didn't report this to anyone?" Lou asked.

"No. I've been scared ever since it happened. I can't eat, sleep, or do my homework. My parents are worried I'm on drugs or have some serious mental-health problem. Maybe I do, but I'm shocked by what I saw and I feel guilty for not saying anything until now. I trust you, so I'm telling you because I know I'll be safe."

"Yes, you're safe, Heather. Was the man with the rifle Mr. Miller?" Lou asked.

"No. I go to high school with his daughter, Charlene, so I know what he looks like."

"Did you see the shooter well enough to describe him? Could you identify him a line-up?"

"I think I could pick him out, especially if I saw him from the side. He was medium height, and as I said, nicely dressed. He didn't have any facial hair. He was going bald, but I wouldn't say he was bald like Mr. Miller."

"What about race or ethnicity?"

"He was not Asian or Hispanic—he looked like you, well, like you, meaning, well, you know what I mean."

"Caucasian?"

"Yeah, that's the word I was groping for."

"Did you see him leave the church?"

"No. I was in the bathroom after the shot and during the commotion. I was scared, and I thought I'd be sick to my stomach."

"I imagine this was very stressful for you and still is," Lou said sympathetically. "I know a therapist who helps people through traumatic situations, and I think it might be helpful for you to talk to her. I think you would like her, and I'm sure she can help you."

"Okay. I know I need somebody's help."

"Have you told your parents what you told me?"

"No. I didn't want to be in the paper and have every kid in school looking at me, thinking about the murder. You're the first person I've told. Should I tell someone?"

"How old are you?"

"Eighteen. I'm a senior in high school."

"You're the age of majority, which means you're independent. I think a meeting between you, me, and your parents would be good. I'm sure they need some answers as to why you've changed your behavior. Did they come to this meeting with you?" Lou asked.

"No. They went to watch my brother play basketball."

"With your permission, I suggest a meeting tomorrow morning. I'll stay overnight in a motel…"

Heather interrupted. "No, my parents should be home from the game. Could you come over now and have this conversation? I'd really like to get it over with."

"Sure. I can do that."

It was ten-thirty when Lou knocked on the Tom's front door. Heather answered and welcomed Lou inside. She introduced him to her parents, Leo and Marjorie. The four went into the living room and sat down.

"Would you like some coffee, Mr. Searing?" Marjorie asked.

"No, thank you. I won't be long."

"Heather says she wants the four of us to discuss something serious," Marjorie said, looking worried. "We're very concerned and afraid for what we might hear."

"I fully understand."

"So, why are you here, Mr. Searing?" Leo asked.

"Heather came to the church this evening. I was invited to brief interested members of the parish on progress, or lack thereof, in finding the killer of Father Dunkel."

"We wanted to go to that, but our son had a basketball game, and we wanted to support him," Marjorie said.

"That's where you belonged! Did he win?" Lou asked.

"No, but he had fun and he's learning fundamental skills," Leo replied.

"That's good. Heather commented during the meeting that she had seen a man come into the church with what appeared to be a tripod case and some camera materials. Afterward she stayed to talk with me. She said she was curious after seeing the man with the camera equipment. Heather tip-toed up a few of the balcony steps, far enough to see the man. He was not setting up a tripod for photographs, but he was positioning a rifle."

"Oh, my God, honey. Oh, how terrifying!" Marjorie said, moving to sit next to Heather, putting her arm around her." I'm so sorry."

"You should've told us, Heather," Leo said lovingly.

"I was scared and almost threw up. Ever since Father Dunkel was shot, I can't get it off my mind."

"You didn't tell us. Did you tell the police? Anyone?" Leo asked in rapid fire order.

"No. But I trust Mr. Searing, and I wanted to tell him."

"She's brave." Lou said with assurance. "I'm proud of her, and we'll protect her."

"I'm so relieved to know why you were upset," Marjorie said holding Heather's hand. "We thought it was that you were pregnant, on drugs, or well, our imaginations just went wild."

Lou sensed an opportunity for Heather. "I suggested to Heather than she see a therapist, and she has agreed. Unless you have a psychiatrist or therapist skilled in trauma, I can recommend a therapist who is experienced and works well with young people."

"We'll take your lead. Do we make an appointment, or will you?" Marjorie asked.

"I'll call and talk to her. Her name is Dr. Choi. I'll ask her to call you so you can visit with her and set up an appointment."

"Does Heather have to talk to the police?" her father asked.

"Not right now. I'll work with the police. They'll not come to your home. You won't have reporters or television crews in your front yard. I recommend Heather begin some therapy and get back on her feet, so to speak. I don't want her or either of you talking to anyone but me about what she saw."

"Okay. Thank you, Mr. Searing," Heather said, relieved.

"You're welcome." Turning to Mr. and Mrs. Toms he said, "You've a brave and conscientious daughter. You can be very proud of her. Now, I'll be on my way. If you have any questions, here's my card. Please don't hesitate to contact me."

Heather gave Lou a hug. As he walked to his car, he turned and saw the three embracing. He had the feeling that all would be well.

Chapter Sixteen

On Thanksgiving morning, Lou called Jack. "I've some news for you on the Dunkel murder."

"Good, because I have news for you, too." Lou then told Jack what he learned from Heather.

"That's great, Lou. I think you're close to solving this. You didn't ask for this, but on my own I've assembled a photo gallery of most of the people you've talked to, who might figure into this murder. I've written each one's name on the back of the photo."

"Great! Thanks, Jack. This is perfect timing, because I now have our first true witness in Heather. If she can point to a photo as the person she saw in the church balcony, we may be close to putting the cuffs on the killer."

"Yes, but if the guy in the balcony is a hired gun, we're back to zero."

"That's right."

Lou contacted Sheriff Kidd using his personal number and relayed the information that exonerated Mark Miller. The sheriff agreed to inform the prosecutor.

"Mark Miller should be released as soon as possible," Lou said with conviction. "He clearly isn't involved. We now know why he couldn't or wouldn't explain his whereabouts that Sunday morning. He truly was not in St. Joseph's Catholic Church."

The prosecutor talked to the judge and asked for immediate release. When the judge learned what others knew, he released Mark, an innocent man, but he knew Mark's incarceration would certainly have an impact on next year's election for prosecutor and circuit judge.

The following Monday, November 28, the headline in the *Traverse City Record-Eagle* read, "Miller Released. New Information Clears Local Man." Mark was pleased to be out of jail. He received calls from a couple of ambulance-chasing lawyers who saw dollar signs in a suit for Mark's damaged reputation and mental anguish.

Mark wasn't the type to seek revenge. He understood the law's mistake and his Christian upbringing wouldn't allow him to seek restitution. And, he realized that his own desire not to explain his whereabouts had led to his arrest. Exonerated, he pledged to the authorities that he would do whatever he could to help find the killer.

One of Mark Miller's first activities after his release was to call the committee, asking them to meet Wednesday evening, November 30.

Mark welcomed everyone with a hug and a smile. "Good to be back. That whole experience was not pleasant. I learned so much!"

"We missed you."

"Thank you. In a state of remorse, our wishing Father Dunkel out of St. Joe's has happened.

"As Janet knows I'm a changed man. There is no room for hatred or judgment of anyone. I was wrong to try to rid our church of Father, and Jesus never would have approved of my thinking or actions. I've gone to confession, but I also ask your forgiveness. We must be able to love, after all, that's all that is real."

The others looked at each other realizing Mark truly was a different person than he had been before Father Dunkel's death.

Chapter Seventeen

Wednesday, November 30, Rae Nix called her husband Gary, who was enjoying a personal retreat at their northern Michigan cottage.

"When are you coming home?" Rae asked.

"I'm selfishly enjoying the peace and quiet. I'll be home soon."

"You're missing all the gossip about the dead priest. Some guy was arrested, but I read that he was released, so the killer is still loose."

"Sounds messy," Gary said.

"It's on the news every night. Ever hear of a detective from Grand Haven named Lou Searing?" Rae asked.

"The name rings a bell. Mystery writer, right?"

"Yes, he investigates murders and then writes books about the cases."

"Why do you mention his name?" Gary asked.

"He's taken on the case. People say he gets his man. So, it looks like the killer will be caught, whoever he is."

"Or she is," Gary corrected Rae. "Don't worry, I'll be home soon."

"I miss you. Kind of hard to believe that you enjoy being without me."

"Please don't go there. I love you, you know that. I'll be home in a day or two, okay?"

"Good. Love you."

Later that morning Carol called to Lou in his second-floor office. "Phone call for you!"

"Thanks!" Lou put the phone to his ear.

"Mr. Searing?"

"Yes."

"This is Gary Nix. I'm calling from my cabin up north."

"Okay. How can I help you?"

"I found you on the Internet and have learned that you're investigating the murder of Albert Dunkel?"

"That's right. Might you be the Dr. Nix who was on the Notre Dame faculty with Dr. Dunkel?"

Yes. I've called because I may be able to help."

"I can always use information."

"You'll come across the name of Tyrone Babcock, a Ph.D. student at Notre Dame about a decade ago. He was denied a Ph.D. degree on a negative vote by his orals committee, of which I was a member. I still have guilty feelings about that vote."

"Excuse me for interrupting, Dr. Nix, but I'm aware of Tyrone."

"Oh, well, that's great. I have some observations for what they're worth."

"They could be worth a lot. Go ahead."

"I'm fairly certain I know who killed Dunkel. It'll probably come as a surprise to you, but it's my opinion none-the-less. I suspect that the murderer was the secretary to the physics department chair at that time. Her name is Marsha Rowden. She was furious when she heard of the injustice to Tyrone."

"Let me get the name again. Marsha, is that M-A-R-C-I-A?"

"No, M-A-R-S-H-A."

"Okay, Marsha Rowden, spelled R-O-W-D-E-N."

"That's correct."

"Well, we're fairly sure the killer is a man. Why would Marsha wait ten years to right this injustice? What makes you believe she killed Dunkel?"

"She has talked about murder ever since she heard about the vote to deny Tyrone his degree. Now that Dr. Dunkel was murdered, it just resonates with me that she's probably his killer."

"Where does she live?"

"She retired from Notre Dame a few years ago. I get a Christmas card from her every year. I'll e-mail you her address."

"I'll look for it and contact her. Anything else you can share?"

"I thought Tyrone handled his disappointment well. He might have been in shock, but whatever the reason, he accepted the decision. He didn't fly out of the room, didn't emit a string of profanities, didn't have a nervous breakdown. He obviously wasn't happy, but he was about as mature as anyone could be in that situation."

"Did anyone make threats on Albert's life at the time?"

"No."

"Any threats on his life since then?"

"Not that I know of."

"Tell me about the other member of the orals committee."

"That would be Dr. Winslow. He was a genius. He had an incredible mind, and a high IQ, but otherwise he seemed to be in La-la Land. He couldn't make a decision. He was a great follower, because he didn't seem to care. He seemed to have no mind of his own. He was a recluse then, and I suspect, if he's still living, he's a recluse now."

"Where was he living the last you heard of him?" Lou asked.

"I lost touch with him when I left Notre Dame. Ask the University Alumni Association about him. He got his doctorate there, and last I heard he was professor emeritus. But, if you ever talk with him, be prepared for an odd duck, although I say that with respect."

Now that Lou knew the man in the front pew was not Mark Miller, the killer's identity remained a mystery Lou was desperate to solve. He contacted the sheriff and asked if he could use the services of an artist from the state police. His request was granted and Lou met with her Thursday, December 1.

"I have two descriptions from different people, Lou began. "The first is that the person is a man, partially bald, no facial hair, no scars or deformities. The second is that the man's profile resembles that of George Washington. So, from these two descriptions can you give me a rendition of what the man might look like?"

"Most definitely. A George Washington profile gives me chin, nose, and forehead. As long as I don't have to draw a wig onto the figure, I can do that quickly. In fact, if you want to wait, I can put something together within the hour."

"Great. I'll wait. This could help crack the case."

"You can watch me draw, or leave and return in about an hour. Your call."

"I'll wait in the reception area. I need to check e-mail and do some reading."

"I'll find you when I've finished."

Forty-five minutes later, the artist appeared in the reception area. She sat down next to Lou holding her sketchbook. "Here's what I've come up with. Look like anyone you know?"

"Can't say that it does, but this will be extremely helpful. I'll talk to people who may have seen the man from various angles."

"The lab technicians can downsize this, and we'll make several copies, so you can leave them with witnesses."

"Thank you. I'm impressed with people like you who have such unique talents."

"Thank you. It's satisfying to know that my talent may bring some justice into this crazy world."

The artist left momentarily and soon returned with an envelope containing copies of her rendition of the man in the front pew.

Armed with the set of photos that Jack gave him plus the artist's drawing, Lou began backtracking to see if anyone he'd met recognized the stranger in the pew.

The first person Lou asked was Heather, whom he had asked to be paged at her high school. Heather looked at each photo and the drawing and then said, "I'm sorry, but I don't recognize anyone. This one might bear a slight resemblance to the man in the balcony, but it's a long shot." Lou turning the photo over saw the name, "Gary Nix" written on the back in Jack's hand-writing.

Next Lou contacted the Wille sisters. They also looked carefully at each photo via e-mail. "This one could be the man in the front row, but I can't be certain," Linda said. Her sisters, Carol and Beth agreed. "Like we said, from the side the man's face had a profile similar to George Washington, and this one has a hint of Washington." Lou thanked the sisters and moved on.

Lou spent the better part of the day chasing down people who may have seen anyone in the photos, meeting with zero success. He hit a brick wall at every meeting.

Call it a detective's intuition, but Lou was fairly sure that none of the Ph.D. students had killed Dr. Dunkel. They may have conspired with someone, but his gut said the three were innocent of murder.

Then Lou showed his set of photos to Father Richards of Saint Patrick's in Yuma. "This guy looks familiar," Father said. "Maybe I just saw his photo in the paper. Yeah, that's probably it, but this photo has meaning to me for some reason." Lou turned the photo over and was surprised to see, "Tim O'Shaughnessy."

Lou found a voice mail message from Heather on his phone. "Mr. Searing, one of my friends from church said she saw 'the cameraman', as we call him, get into a car. She knows the car because her parents have the same make and model. If you want to talk to her, please call me."

Lou called Heather, thanked her, and noted the contact information for her friend, Kaylee Herbert. He called Kaylee.

"Hello, Kaylee?"

"Yes."

"This is Lou Searing. I've been investigating the murder of Father Dunkel. Heather says you saw something that might help."

"Yeah, I saw the photographer get in a car and drive away."

"You say 'the photographer'. How did you know he was a photographer?"

"He had the tripod case, a camera bag, and a camera around his neck."

"What kind of car did he drive?"

"It was a Honda SUV—new, blue."

"Did you see a license number?"

"No."

"Thank you, Kaylee."

Lou knew that, as predictably as people sat in the same pews, they often parked their cars in the same places.

Because Marilyn and Ken Malkowski usually park where the Honda was seen, Lou called and asked them if they saw the blue Honda SUV that morning.

"Yes, we saw it and remarked on it," Ken said.

"Did you note a license plate?"

"Yes, actually. It was an Indiana plate—letters WMST, but I don't know the numbers. We remembered the letters because it reminded us of where we used to live, Williamston."

"Did you see the driver of the car, either before or after Mass?"

"No."

"Were there any passengers?"

"Can't help you there," Ken said.

"Did you see any decals in the windows or on the bumper?" Lou asked.

"No. Well, wait a minute, yes we did. There was a Notre Dame decal in the back window. We said, 'probably a Catholic kid home on vacation'."

"Thank you, Mr. Malkowski."

"You're welcome. Glad I could help."

Lou was pleased to be making some progress. He would have liked to have the license number, but he was thankful for what he had.

Lou called Jack for more help. "Jack, could you please contact the Indiana Motor Vehicles Department? I need the number of licenses beginning with the letters 'WMST'. Then ask if I can get the names of drivers who have those four letters on their plates."

"I'm on it, Lou."

"One more thing, please."

"Sure."

"I need to know what cars are driven by everyone in the set of photos you gave me, plus any of their license numbers."

"Sounds like you're onto something, Lou."

"Getting close, I hope."

"Good."

Chapter Eighteen

Three days after she talked with Gary; Rae called him again, hoping he might be on his way home. When Gary didn't answer, she called Ned's Bar. "Ned, have you seen Gary?"

"Not in the past couple of days. He's a regular when he's up here. I just assumed he went home."

"He's not here, and he doesn't answer his phone."

"Do you want me to go to the cabin and see if I can find him?"

"Thanks, Ned. I'd really appreciate that. I'm thinking the worst."

"Relax, I'll find him," Ned said, hoping he wouldn't find Gary hanging from a pine tree.

Ned told his bartender he would be gone for about an hour. "Call me on my cell if you need me."

Ned drove the ten miles to the Nix driveway, pulled in and drove to the cabin. Gary's car was there, so Ned knew he should be around. Pulling to a stop, he blew his car horn a few times, expecting Gary to appear from the cabin or the nearby shed.

When there was no response, Ned walked to the front of the

cottage, where he found the curtains drawn. Glancing in the direction of the dock, he saw Gary's rowboat. All appeared normal, except that Gary was missing.

Ned walked to the door and rapped on it, shouting, "Hey, Nix, you here?" There was no response.

Ned began to think the worst. With the boat and car at the cabin, Gary should be there unless he'd taken a hike and fallen. Any number of things could have happened.

The door was unlocked since there was usually no reason to lock the cabin. Ned turned the handle, cracked the door, and once again shouted, "Nix? You here, man?"

Silence. Ned stepped in expecting to find Gary dead, but he wasn't in the cabin. No note explained his absence. Ned noted ashes in the fireplace, but he couldn't tell how long ago a fire had been lit. There didn't appear to have been a struggle, nor did anything appear to have been stolen.

Ned decided to walk around the wood pile near the cabin to see if he could spot Gary. He saw no one, so he went to the waterfront to see if there were footprints heading into the water but not coming back out indicating a possible drowning. He didn't find anything amiss.

Thinking he'd done all he could to find Gary, Ned got back in his car and headed to his bar. En route he called Rae and told her what he had found.

"Thanks, Ned. I'll drive up. This is strange. If you see him or hear anything about him, please give me a call."

"I sure hope everything is okay."

"Thanks. I'll stop in to see you and report whatever I find."

"Okay, have a safe trip."

PERISH PRIEST

Rae Nix drove to their cabin in the woods outside of Baldwin, Michigan, on December 3. She felt certain Gary had met with some catastrophe. As she pulled in the drive, she noted that his car was not parked by the cabin. She was puzzled, because Ned had said Gary's car was at the cottage. As she got out of her car, she noticed that the back door was open. It was always unlocked, but it was usually closed. She glanced toward the shore and saw the boat floating aimlessly, the chain that secured it to the dock loosened.

She cautiously went into the cabin. Empty beer bottles were strewn around the kitchen. This was odd because Gary didn't drink beer. She thought, *Maybe kids got in here and had a party, but why is Gary missing?*

In the bedroom, other than the bed not being made, everything looked normal. The bathroom appeared normal, also. She then went into the TV room which had easy chairs. This too looked normal, except the channel being viewed when the TV had been turned off was a movie channel. She knew that, while he was at the cabin, all Gary ever watched were the golf channel and ESPN.

Hearing a car in the driveway, she looked out the back window. The county sheriff got out of a squad car with gun drawn and walked toward the cabin. Rae went out to meet the guest because she didn't want to surprise him.

Without greeting her he asked, "You alone?"

"Yes. What's wrong?"

"Are you Mrs. Nix?"

"Yes. Is Gary all right?"

"He should be. Bunch of drunken kids beat him up pretty bad."

"Where is he?" Rae asked, upset at this news.

"He received severe blows to the head, so he's been taken to Munson Hospital in Traverse City."

"Oh, my God. This is terrible. I've got to get there."

"I'll have one of my deputies drive you up there in your car."

"That would be wonderful. Thank you!"

"Leave the cottage the way it is. I'll need to collect evidence. I'll lock it. Meanwhile, come with me, and I'll call a deputy and we'll get you to your husband."

"Thank you."

Dr. Nix was being tended to by paramedics in the ambulance. While they were in contact with the trauma team at Munson Hospital, he faded in and out of consciousness. The paramedics were doing exactly what they were trained to do.

Rae was thankful she didn't have to drive. With Gary and the strange circumstances on her mind, she felt like she could pass out at any moment.

When the deputy and Rae arrived at the hospital, Gary was in surgery. Three brain surgeons were working on him. They first relieved the pressure and then gave him drugs to combat infection. Part of his skull was cut away, and his head was in a halo brace basically immobilizing his head.

In the ER waiting room, Rae signed admitting papers and was examined and given a green light, meaning she didn't need medical attention for her emotional distress. Presently, she was briefed regarding Gary's surgery. Once she realized there was nothing she could do, she called her best friend who immediately set out for Traverse City. A couple of other friends were on standby, should she need anything.

Rae called her children wanting to tell them herself instead of them hearing the news from a police officer or reporter. They were numbed by the news. Their son in South Bend, Indiana, and their daughter in Chicago made plans to get to Traverse City as soon as possible.

Lou felt fairly confident that the killer was the driver of the blue Honda with Indiana plates. Once he connected this vehicle with a person, he would likely have the murderer.

Lou contacted Dr. Winslow in Chicago.

"Dr. Winslow? Lou Searing here."

"Ah, the private eye. Got your killer yet?"

"Gaining on him, actually."

"You must have another question."

"What kind of car do you drive?" Lou asked.

"I don't drive."

"How do you get around?"

"I don't need a car in Chicago—there's plenty of public transportation."

"I see. Were you in Michigan during the past couple of months?"

"Nope, I've been in Chicago for a couple of years, but I've gone to a couple of Notre Dame football games in South Bend—I take Amtrak there and back."

"Do you know anyone who owns a blue Honda SUV?"

"Can't say that I do. Sorry."

"Thanks for talking with me, Dr. Winslow."

Jack used a service that had been helpful previously and was definitely worth the cost. The service alerted him whenever a specific name or names were posted on the Internet. His attention perked up when he saw an alert on his computer screen: "Happening Now! Distinguished Boston College Professor Beaten by Thugs. Dr. Gary Nix has been taken to Munson Hospital in Traverse City." The report told of a man who, while staying at his cabin in northern Michigan, was apparently robbed at gunpoint and then driven in his car to a desolate area and beaten. There were two photos of cars in the story; one was a county sheriff vehicle, and the other was a dark SUV, which looked to Jack like a Toyota or a Honda.

Jack immediately relayed the information to Lou who put Munson Hospital into his GPS and headed for Traverse City.

Lou arrived and parked in the visitor lot. Encountering Rae in the surgery waiting room, he introduced himself and expressed his sadness at the tragedy that had come to the Nix family.

"I don't know if your husband mentioned me to you but I'm investigating the murder of Father Dunkel. I don't know whether you knew him or not."

"Oh yes, I knew Albert," Rae replied. "In fact, I was one of the few faculty wives who sort of liked him. Believe me; it was hard to like that man! He probably displayed a bit of every kind of mental health problem in the book. In fact, if I were going to describe him, I'd put the word 'little' before every major mental health concept. You know, a little schizoid, a little paranoid, a little neurotic, a little bipolar. When you put all the 'littles' together, you get a man with problems."

"I had talked to your husband about Dr. Dunkel and also a colleague, Dr. Winslow…"

"Oh yes, Reggie. He's his own crazy self, in my opinion. He was, or still is, a weak man: A mama's boy, a guy with no backbone, easily swayed to anyone's way of thinking. I'm surprised he survived in the dog-eat-dog world of academia."

Lou nodded. "And, of course, I've talked to the three Ph.D. students who were denied the degree because of a vote of their committee, which in each case was made up of your husband, Dr. Dunkel, and Dr. Winslow."

"Sad, very sad. You get to know these young, brilliant students well. They have seminars in our homes. They almost become your children while they're earning their degrees. It ripped my heart out when those three were denied their Ph.D.s. In fact, I can't think of a greater injustice."

"Anyway, I'm working to find who killed Dr. Dunkel. But, more important at the moment is your husband. What can you tell me?"

"I don't know much, actually. He didn't respond to my calls, so I called the bar where he usually has his happy hour, but they hadn't seen him. Ned, the bar owner, drove out to the cabin, but he couldn't find him, even though his car was there and things appeared normal.

"I decided to drive up. When I arrived I saw that the cabin had been ransacked, there were beer cans all over, and the car was gone. Right then the sheriff arrived with the news that Gary had been robbed and beaten by thugs. He told me Gary had been taken to Munson Hospital. He offered me a ride, and here I am."

"I see. Where do you live in Michigan?"

"We have an apartment in Boston, where Gary is on the graduate faculty of Boston College. Then we have a small home in Ithaca, about 35 or so miles north of Lansing. And, our cottage is near Baldwin."

"Three homes to keep up—quite a chore, I imagine," Lou said.

"Well, this is a bone of contention. I never wanted the expense or responsibility for another place, but Gary said he needed a quiet place for his mental health. So, we got a good deal on the cabin—bought it a couple of years ago. I'll admit that it's a quiet setting, but now that this has happened, I'm sure I'll never go there again."

"What have the doctors told you about his condition?" Lou asked.

"Brain injury is the biggest concern. He's got broken bones and some lacerations, but they'll heal. They've inserted a stent in his brain to keep pressure from building up and to drain any excess fluid. He wasn't conscious when he went into surgery. Of course they want me to be upbeat, but I must be realistic, prepare for possible bad news. He could even die from this." Tears appeared in Rae's eyes. "Maybe I'm selfish, but I know Gary would not want to live a life where he couldn't teach or enjoy his cabin. We'll have to wait and see."

"Are you Catholic?" Lou asked. "Has a priest been here yet?"

"No, we're not Catholic. In fact, we're atheists. Gary is probably the only atheist faculty member at any Catholic university. When asked, he proudly boasts of his non-belief."

"How long do they expect him to be in surgery?"

"They couldn't give me a precise time. They expect it to be hours, but of course, nobody knows."

"Can you go to the cafeteria, or would you rather stay here?"

"I'd rather stay here. Our children are expected within a few hours, and I want to be here when they arrive."

"I understand. Where are they from?"

Our son, Brian, is from Indiana. He works at Notre Dame—administration office. Our daughter, Becky is from Chicago. She's an accountant there. Brad lives in Germany. He works for the State Department in Berlin. He won't be able to come here. I'm keeping him informed by skype."

"Is anyone else coming to be with you?"

"I think a friend is coming, but I don't know when she'll arrive."

"I'm going to the cafeteria for a bite. Do you want me to bring you something?" Lou asked.

"That's very kind of you. I'd like a sandwich and a diet drink of some kind."

"I'll be back soon."

"Thank you, Mr. Searing."

"Call me Lou."

"Thank you, Lou."

Lou went to the cafeteria and purchased items for Rae, then decided to eat his own food in the cafeteria. He needed a little peace and quiet. While eating his burger, his cell phone rang. It was Jack.

"Lou, are you at Munson yet?" Jack asked.

"Yes, have been here about a half-hour."

"You asked me to show the photographs to the church organist. She says the man in the first pew was definitely Tim O'Shaughnessy. She says she was wrong about the man being Mark Miller, but that she honestly believed the man to be Mr. Miller."

"Interesting. I thought O'Shaughnessy was never out of sight of the administrator at Ferris State."

"It may not be him, but she has positively identified O'Shaughnessy, the failed Ph.D. student."

"Thanks, Jack. I'm talking with Gary Nix's wife, Rae, and trying to be supportive during this stressful time."

When Lou got back to the waiting room, Rae was napping, which was undoubtedly good for her physical and mental health. Lou sat down and waited for her to wake up and have her food.

Brian and Becky had arrived, looking tired, upset, and concerned. She greeted them with warm hugs and a few tears. This was a time for family, so Lou slipped out of the waiting area.

When Lou returned to the lounge, a nurse had approached Rae and children. "Your husband is stable and the surgery is going well."

"Thank God!" Rae said. Lou thought that a bit odd for an atheist, but… "Will he live?" Rae asked.

"It's too early to tell the extent of his injuries. Everything is going as planned. The surgeons expect a couple more hours of surgery, and then he'll be in recovery. You can expect him to remain in the hospital for several weeks. Do you need help finding accommodations? If so, a social worker will assist you."

"Thank you very much."

"You're welcome." She shook hands with Brian and Becky. She didn't greet Lou, which was fine, but Lou thought it a bit odd in that he could've been a family member as well.

Rae suggested that her children go to the cafeteria. She would remain in the waiting area and eat her sandwich.

On occasion because of his reasoning or intuition, Jack will act without asking Lou's permission. It doesn't happen often but Jack felt safe in what he wanted to do, so he proceeded. He called the sheriff's office in Lake County, asking to speak to someone who could give him an update of a criminal act.

"Are you a reporter?"

"No. I work with Lou Searing, a private detective who is currently working on the case of the murdered priest in Mesick."

"One moment, please."

"This is Officer Hilker. What do you need?"

"For the record, my name is Jack Kelly and I'm assisting Lou Searing in the investigation of the murder of Father Dunkel in Mesick, Michigan."

"Okay. What do you need?"

"Dr. Gary Nix, the man who was robbed and beaten near Baldwin. Could you describe the Nix vehicle?"

"Dark blue late-model Honda SUV, Indiana license WMST 488."

"What was found in the car?" Jack asked.

"A rifle with silencer, a couple of cameras, and a camera bag. We also found a small suitcase with toiletries and dirty clothes."

"Thank you. Finally, is there a Notre Dame decal on the back window, lower right?"

"Yes."

"Thank you for your help. Here's my phone number in case the sheriff or anyone else needs to verify my affiliation with Mr. Searing."

"That won't be necessary, but thanks, Mr. Kelly," said Officer Hilker.

Jack called Lou, who left the waiting area before he took the call. "What have you got, Jack?"

"The dark blue Honda SUV belongs to Dr. Nix."

"Interesting," Lou replied. "Nix could be our shooter, and Tim for whatever reason, could have been sitting in the front pew."

"If they're working together, Tim could have been there to take the brunt of the crowd while Nix calmly left the church," Jack reasoned.

"But they didn't wrestle him to the floor and hold him till the cops came," Lou replied.

"Right, so he probably left with Nix."

"Nix must have taken him to Big Rapids and then either went home to Ithaca or went to his cabin," Lou explained. "This is an interesting development. We may have the main characters in this case, but we still need to rule out others and find a motive."

"I know I acted without your knowledge, Lou. If I was out of line, I'm sorry. But, I wanted to follow up on a hunch and didn't think you would mind."

"Jack, I trust your instincts and your judgment to know when to act and when not to. I'll contact the sheriff and explain what we know."

"Okay. Let me know if there's anything else I can do."

"I will. I'll be staying in the Traverse City area tonight. I'm too tired to drive to Grand Haven."

"Sounds like a plan."

At half past eleven the surgery was over. The team of doctors invited Rae and the children to join them in a conference area. The head surgeon spoke. "It was a long time in surgery. His injuries were profound. We really can't give you hope for a full recovery, but we want you to be positive."

"Is he alert?" Rae asked.

"He's in recovery right now and we don't know if or when he might regain consciousness. Staff is keeping an eye on him."

"Can we see him?" Becky asked.

"We'll require that you put on scrubs and then go in one at a time. Please do not stay long."

"Will he know we are there?" Brian asked.

"It's hard to tell. He may and he may not. But, we'd like you to talk to him."

"I assume the next several hours are critical?" Rae said, dabbing her eyes with a Kleenex.

"Yes, definitely. One of our main concerns is infection. The other is whether his heart can take this attack and the several hours of surgery."

"Thank you, Doctor," Brian said, shaking the doctor's hand. "We appreciate all that you've done for him."

"You're welcome. Someone from our team will give you periodic briefings. Be sure the receptionist knows how to reach you, and also tell her if you plan to stay in the area tonight."

"We will. Thank you again."

Dr. Nix died at 3:47 on the morning of Dec. 4. Apparently, his heart couldn't withstand the assault on his body. No action was taken as Rae had signed a do-not-resuscitate order. Lou participated in a family hug at the hospital and stayed with the grief-stricken family for a couple of hours.

Lou called Jack to tell him of Nix's death. He also called the sheriff to inform him of developments—that the murderer appeared to be Gary Nix and for some reason, Tim O'Shaughnessy, had been in the front pew. More research was to follow.

Lou went home mid-morning, very tired, for the previous day and night had been taxing. Once he relaxed, he called Paul Wright, the head of the science department at Ferris State.

"Mr. Searing. It is good to hear from you."

"Thank you. I have a couple of questions for you."

"Certainly."

"You said when we talked that Tim lives with you, and that he hasn't left your sight for a couple of years, or words to that effect."

"That's what I said, and it's the truth."

"I'm fairly certain that Tim was sitting in Mesick's St. Joseph's Catholic Church the morning of October 30. Were you with him?"

"No, I wasn't. I guess I have to admit that there are some occasions when I allow him to go somewhere with a friend, or with someone I know."

"Do you know Gary Nix?"

"I don't believe so."

"How do you explain Tim being in St. Joseph's church in Mesick?"

"Who was he with?"

"I can't be certain he was with anyone. He could've been with Dr. Nix, but I can't be certain of that."

"Who is this Dr. Nix?" Paul asked.

"Gary Nix was on Tim's Ph.D. dissertation committee at Notre Dame when he was denied his degree."

"Oh, Gary. Yes. I know Gary. I never learned his last name. Sorry. Yes, Gary takes Tim on an occasional outing. Gary's from Boston, right?"

"Right."

"He has a home in Michigan. He wants to stay in touch with Tim. I trust him, and I allow Tim to go with him."

"Do you know whether they may have gone to St. Joseph's the morning of October 30?"

"I don't ask Gary where they're going or where they've been. As I said, I trust him."

"Did Tim say anything about going to St. Joseph's?" Lou asked.

"No. He never tells me about his outings with Gary and I don't ask. I figure the man needs some privacy."

"Is he with you right now?"

"He's in his room."

"Would you ask him if he went with Gary to St. Joseph's Church?"

"Sure. Hang on."

Three long minutes later, Dr. Wright came back on the phone.

"He says he was with Gary in that church."

"Did he say why?"

"He says they went to see Dr. Dunkel."

"Did he say anything about what happened there?"

"No, he keeps looking down and won't say a word."

"Let me put you on guard here. The police will likely come to talk to Tim and you."

"Is he in trouble?" Paul asked.

"He may have witnessed the murder of Dr. Dunkel. I tell you this so you can prepare to have an attorney with you, and perhaps a mental-health worker to assist in questioning Tim."

"Are you suggesting that Dr. Nix killed Dr. Dunkel?"

"He's definitely a suspect."

"Thank you, Mr. Searing. This is shocking. I can't imagine Gary harming anyone, and I certainly can't imagine Tim being involved unless he was forced to do something against his will."

Dr. Wright would contact legal counsel for Ferris State asking for a meeting as soon as possible. An attorney, Lisa Moylan would come to Paul's home in about an hour. Lou wanted to be present so he drove to Big Rapids.

When Lisa, Tim, Paul, and Lou were gathered, Lisa began, "Tim, I need you to tell me the truth. OK?" Tim nodded.

"Were you present in St. Joseph's Church when Dr. Dunkel was shot?"

"Yes, I was."

"Who shot him?"

"I don't know. I didn't hear a shot. Father Dunkel fell forward and was on the floor. Gary told me to sit in the front row, and if people screamed, I was to get up and go to his car. That's what I did."

"What did Gary say when you two drove away from the church?"

"I don't remember for sure. He brought me back home. I don't remember what we talked about."

"Was Gary carrying anything when you went into the church?"

"Cameras. He had a bunch of photo stuff. I asked him why he had all the cameras and stuff."

"What did he say, Tim?"

"I don't remember for sure, I think he just said he was taking shots, something like that, I guess."

"So you didn't know the priest was killed?"

"No."

"Did Gary seem nervous, anxious, or worried?"

"I don't know."

"He drove you home, and then what?" Lou asked.

"I don't know. He said he'd visit again sometime. I said 'Bye' and he drove away."

"The police will be coming to talk to you, Tim. You need to tell them what you've told us. Do you understand?" Lou asked.

"Am I in trouble?"

"No, you're not in trouble," Lou said. But it's important that you answer the questions truthfully."

"Okay. I will. Gary's in trouble, isn't he?"

"He could be, Tim. We can't draw any conclusions."

The next evening, Lou and Carol took their evening walk along the beach. Unlike in summer, when T-shirts and shorts were comfortable, this evening called for winter coats, wool caps, and warm boots. These walks were a time when the two would share things on their mind. For Lou, it was a quiet time to benefit from Carol's insights into the case.

"I'm pretty sure who pulled the trigger and who was in the front row. Mark Miller's been cleared."

"You never thought he was a viable suspect anyway, did you?" Carol asked.

"No. It would've been freakish at best."

"So who's the shooter?" Carol asked.

"The question is, who <u>was</u> the shooter?"

"Whatever. Who killed the priest?"

"Unless I find evidence to the contrary, the killer was Dr. Gary Nix."

"Was the killer?" Carol asked, confused.

"Yes, the killer died in Traverse City a couple of nights ago."

"Who was he?"

"A professor of physics at Notre Dame when Dr. Dunkel was there."

"Why did he kill Dunkel?"

"We may never know. He took the motive to his grave."

"Did he have an accomplice?" Carol asked, sounding like a reporter.

"Tim O'Shaughnessy was with him, but I don't know what role he played, if any."

"Who is Tim?" Carol asked.

"He was a doctoral candidate in physics at Notre Dame. He's mentally ill, lives with an administrator at Ferris State in Big Rapids."

"So, the case is closed? Lock it up and throw away the key?"

"Not quite," Lou replied. "I need to see if any other suspects were involved, and I'm hoping to come up with a motive that's plausible."

The couple turned and began the half-mile walk back to their home.

Chapter Nineteen

Two of the Ph.D. committee were now dead, Lou mused. Dr. Winslow was alive, but he had Alzheimer's. Lou called him to touch base.

"Dr. Winslow, this is Lou Searing, the detective looking into the murder of Dr. Dunkel."

"Okay, have we ever met?"

"A couple of times."

"I'm sorry, I don't recall."

"Do you remember when you were a professor at Notre Dame?"

"Yes, vaguely."

"Do you remember the names Gary Nix and Albert Dunkel?"

"Should I know them?"

"You were on the graduate physics faculty with them."

Just then, another person came on the phone. "This is Dr. Winslow's caregiver, Jonathon. Why are you calling?"

"My name is Lou Searing, and I'm a private investigator from

Michigan looking into the murder of Dr. Dunkel, a colleague of Dr. Winslow's at Notre Dame."

"Dr. Winslow isn't going to be much help."

"I understand that. I've talked with him a couple of times."

"Why are you calling now?" Jonathon asked.

"Because Dr. Dunkel and Dr. Nix have both died, and I'm wondering if Dr. Winslow was involved."

"I'm sure he wasn't. His memory is going fast. I see changes every day now. I'm sure he remembers nothing that can help you, and I'm also sure he is not involved. Thank you for calling. Good-bye." Jonathan hung up.

Lou wasn't ready to end the call and didn't appreciate the conversation coming to an abrupt end, but what happened, happened. He put his phone in his pocket.

Lou turned his attention to the three students, wondering whether they had played any part in the crime. He first contacted Jennifer Kale. "I'm assuming you've heard that Dr. Nix is dead," he began.

"No, I didn't know that."

"He was severely beaten at his cottage up north. He survived brain surgery, but died a few hours afterward."

"I'm sorry to hear that. He was a wonderful advocate for students. He was quite upset when the three of us didn't get the degrees we had earned."

"I'm sorry to give you this news."

"Thank you for calling. Has the murder of Dr. Dunkel been solved?"

"Not quite."

"I'm thinking Dr. Nix might have something to do with it," Jennifer said.

"Why do you say that?" Lou asked.

"Drs. Nix and Dunkel never got along, but then nobody, student or faculty, really got along with Dr. Dunkel."

"What was the problem between them?"

"Dr. Dunkel was a reviewer for a prestigious journal. When he received an article written by Dr. Nix, word is that Dunkel gave the manuscript a poor review which was the reason the article wasn't accepted for publication. Dr. Nix was furious. The manuscript should never have gone to Dunkel because they worked at the same university, and Dunkel should have declined the request to review it. Anyway, after that, there was little if any interaction between Nix and Dunkel."

"Let me be precise, and I'll state this positively: None of you three Ph.D. students were involved in killing Fr. Dunkel."

"Ty and I were not. I was not involved, and I'm ninety-nine percent sure Ty wasn't. Tim,—I don't know. We haven't communicated since our Ph.D. study."

"Okay. Thanks."

"I hope you can solve this, Mr. Searing."

"I'm closing in. It shouldn't be much longer."

Lou explained all he knew to the sheriff. "I'd like to go to Boston to search Nix's office at Boston College. Is that possible?"

"I'll notify the authorities there that Dr. Nix is a suspect who has died, and you wish to search the office, looking for evidence of a motive or conspirators. This kind of request is common. I'm sure they'll agree."

"I'd like access to his computer and his files. I also want to be able to study any papers on his desk or on shelves. I pretty much want the right to look at everything I think relevant."

"I understand."

"I'll take Jack Kelly with me. The two of us can conduct the search."

"I'll handle permission and any paper work needed to give you access to his office. You can plan your trip. Unless you get a call from me, you should be free to go later this afternoon."

Carol was delighted with the invitation to go to Boston, for she had not been there in several years. It would be a nice break from her routine in Grand Haven. Jack Kelly declined because of a church commitment. So, Lou and Carol packed clothes and needed items for a couple of days.

They flew from Grand Rapids to Detroit, and then on to Boston, landing at Logan International Airport on a perfect early December day. They hailed two cabs; Lou was headed for Boston College, and Carol would check in at the hotel and set out for the stores.

With a valise in hand, Lou walked into the physics building and asked to speak to the chairperson. The administrator wasn't in, but the secretary knew Lou was coming. She took Lou to Gary's office, unlocked the door and said, "Let me know if there's anything you need."

"Thank you."

Where to begin, Lou thought. He sat behind Nix's desk, took a deep breath and wondered how to proceed, so as not to waste time but to find the information he needed.

The office was filled with books and file cabinets. It was an office where the professor who claimed it as his spot on earth knew where everything was. But most strangers would call it a mess.

Lou decided the books covering the walls needn't be searched. He opened file cabinets and found nothing of interest. A file drawer labeled 'correspondence' caught Lou's eye. Maybe something in this file would yield information.

For the next three hours, through four cups of coffee, Lou found nothing of interest. Before he left for the day, he asked for a technician to help him get into Nix's computer so he could search for e-mails and icons that might yield information. He told the receptionist he'd be back in the morning. He found nothing at the end of the first day.

Lou and Carol went to dinner at a nice restaurant. Afterward, they walked around, people-watching and browsing through interesting stores. They were early risers, so it was soon back to the hotel and to bed.

The next morning, Lou and Carol shared breakfast in their hotel. "How long will you be today?" Carol asked.

"Hard to tell. I found nothing yesterday, and it might be the same today—or I might hit a gold mine. Make sure your cell phone is on. I'll let you know as the day progresses."

"We're on a flight leaving at 6:10 this evening," Carol reminded Lou.

"If I don't find anything by mid-afternoon, I suspect I'll call the search unsuccessful. I'll call you so we can make arrangements to get to the airport."

"Sounds good. I'll check out of the hotel and leave our luggage with the porter."

Lou took a cab to Boston College and greeted the receptionist, who again escorted him to Dr. Nix's office. "As before, let me know if you need anything."

"I might need papers copied. Do I ask you for help with that, or should I talk to someone else?"

"Let me know what you need," the student receptionist replied.

The rest of the morning was like a wild-goose chase. Lou found a few items from Nix's time at Notre Dame, but nothing like what he'd hoped to find.

The professor whose office was next to Dr. Nix's stopped in and spoke briefly with Lou. "I'm David Zuckerman. I'm going to the faculty lounge for a sandwich and drink. Can I get you something?"

"That would be great. Thank you."

"I'll be back in about twenty minutes."

When the professor returned with lunch, Lou asked, "Who knew Dr. Nix best?"

"That would be me."

"Lou Searing is my name." The two shook hands.

"Yes. The chairman sent the faculty an e-mail explaining that you would be visiting for a couple of days."

"Did Dr. Nix ever mention a Doctor or Father Dunkel?"

"He referred to him once. He didn't like him, as I recall."

"Did he make any threatening comments directed toward Dunkel?"

"No. He simply said a colleague at Notre Dame was a terrible human being. I recall him saying this man was the reason a few scholars didn't pass their orals several years ago."

"Yes, I'm familiar with all of that."

"He said something recently which I thought was positive. He had petitioned the president of Notre Dame, or maybe the dean of graduate studies—I'm not sure. Anyway, he made a case for Notre Dame issuing the Ph.D. degree to those students from years ago. They had done exemplary research, and they deserved the degree. He also suggested that the University make financial awards in an attempt to compensate them for their subsequent losses in income."

"That's most kind," Lou replied. "My guess is the petition would be denied. I can't imagine giving a degree years after a decision to deny it."

"I agree, but I give Gary credit for trying to correct a wrong."

"True. But did he ever make a threatening statement about this Dr. Dunkel, either seriously or in jest?"

"He never said anything that could be construed as a threat, no."

Chapter Twenty

L ou looked through files and correspondence, finding nothing. He
was just about to call Carol when his eyes fell on a letter from the
dean of sciences at Notre Dame, dated October 1. He read,

Dear Dr. Nix,

*Your scholarly letter of July 7 has been studied by chosen
members of our physics department. Based on their study and
recommendations, we will take steps to award the Ph.D. degree
to Tyrone Babcock, along with a monetary award of twenty-five
thousand dollars in lost wages. We thank you for submitting the
work of Mr. Babcock and for presenting supporting information to
give credence to his work and conclusions.*

*We have reviewed Jennifer Kale's dissertation of 2005 and
also found a grievous error in denying her a Ph.D. degree for her
research. She will receive the degree and the same monetary award.
We will contact both Mr. Babcock and Jennifer Kale to present their
degrees and financial awards for damages to their career.*

*Regarding Tim O'Shaughnessy, I have asked a committee to
review his research and recommend a course of action. I expect they
will agree that Mr. O'Shaughnessy's work warrants a Ph.D. degree,
but a decision has not been made as of this date.*

The faculty and I are indebted to you for helping us reverse a wrong. You will be receiving a letter of commendation from the president of Notre Dame.

Sincerely,

Sandra Montgomery, Chair, Department of Physics, Notre Dame University.

Attached was a letter written to Father Dunkel from Dr. Nix. It was dated June 20. It read:

Dear Albert,

After many years of guilt and anger, I've come to the conclusion that we were involved in a grave injustice to three doctoral candidates in 2005. I'm sure you know of whom I speak. I propose to draft a letter to the dean suggesting that our vote be overturned and the degree be conferred upon each. Further, I'll suggest that some reasonable amount of money be awarded to each representing lost wages during the past decade.

The purpose of this letter is to ask your approval. As a man of God, I'm sure that you're bothered by our actions. We basically ruined the careers of three brilliant scientists.

Please let me know your thoughts. Assuming you concur, I'll take action immediately.

Sincerely,

Dr. Gary Nix

Attached to this letter was a letter in reply from Albert, dated June 29. It read:

> *Dear Gary,*
>
> *Have you lost your mind? Do you realize what this would say about us as scientists? It admits we were wrong in the action we took. Even worse, it would imply that we erred in other decisions. If we do this, every student we ever dismissed would have a basis to appeal.*
>
> *I will not support your idea, and, if you proceed, I will use whatever influence I have to kill this. Your reputation will be significantly harmed. To use a common phrase, this will only happen "OVER MY DEAD BODY!"*
>
> *I trust Rae is well. Please give her my regards. I always liked and respected her.*
>
> *Sincerely,*
>
> *Albert Dunkel*

Lou couldn't help but notice that someone, and undoubtedly, Dr. Nix, took a red magic marker and highlighted "Over my dead body!" A blue pen was used to write, "Your wish is my command!"

Lou called Carol. "I found the needle in the haystack. Case closed. This will be the happiest flight I've ever enjoyed because, a) I'm with you, and b) because the murder of Albert Dunkel has been solved."

While waiting for their luggage at the Gerald R. Ford International Airport, Lou called Alex Halley at the *Traverse City Record-Eagle*. "I'm a man of my word. I will soon give the sheriff and the prosecutor a report that specifies that Dr. Gary Nix was the killer of Dr. Dunkel. Call me in a few hours, and I will share the particulars. I need to call the sheriff now."

Alex was delighted. "Thank you, Mr. Searing. You are a gentleman!"

Epilogue

Dr. Tyrone Babcock was thankful for Dr. Nix's recommendation and to the University of Notre Dame for the cash award. His degree hangs proudly in his home.

Dr. Kale decided to keep her degree hidden. She feared that whenever she saw the diploma or someone called her Dr. Kale, it would bring back the bad memories and the bitter feelings she held toward Dr. Dunkel. She preferred her life without the title after her name or the framed degree hanging on the wall.

Dr. Tim O'Shaughnessy never understood what was happening. The degree hung on a wall in his Big Rapids apartment, but he comprehended neither what it was nor what it represented.

Dr. Winslow was incapable of understanding what Notre Dame had done for three students denied a Ph.D. degree in 2005. Reggie is on the waiting list to reside in a memory-challenged facility in Chicago.

Bishop Grether was thankful the threats had ceased, for he could address other important issues in his diocese. He was the celebrant for Father Dunkel's funeral Mass. The church was full and in the congregation were many priests and almost every member of the St. Joseph's parish. Within six months of the funeral, he made the decision to close St. Joseph's asking Father Richards and St. Patrick's in Yuma to accept responsibility for the parishioners of St. Joseph.

Mrs. Bosseker, the church organist at St. Joseph couldn't bring herself to sit at the organ given the vivid memory of Father Dunkel's tragic death. She never entered St. Joseph's again.

Heather Toms received therapy and gradually became her old self. She was given an award for public service in supporting Mr. Searing in investigating a crime. She is thinking of majoring in Forensic Science at Michigan State University.

Joseph Windemere was the man Mark Miller was counseling the morning Father Dunkel was shot. Following the murder and before Mark's arrest, Joe left for Africa where he was volunteering for Habitat for Humanity. He had no family to send him news of Mark's being in jail. Joe didn't return home till the murder was solved.

Ted Owens was denied acceptance to a seminary because of a confidential problem. Father Dunkel recommended he not be allowed to become a priest because of what he had heard in the confessional. He could not reveal what he had heard about Teddy's problem so he simply informed the bishop that Teddy was not an acceptable candidate for the priesthood and that was that.

Both the circuit judge and the prosecutor were defeated on election day. Sheriff Kidd, however, was reelected by a wide margin.

Mrs. Nix sold the cabin in Northern Michigan. She moved to a condo on Cape Cod and enjoys living among the wealthy.

Jack Kelly's joy came from helping Lou solve another mystery. Justice being served was all the thanks he needed.

Carol Searing was thankful that Lou had successfully solved another murder and remained healthy. She could only hope Lou would sooner than later give up his unquenchable thirst for bringing justice to others. Only time will tell.

Lou Searing filed his report and then began writing his book about this case. He titled it <u>Perish Priest </u>and wondered how many times he would need to explain that 'Perish' was not misspelled.

The End

Postscript

There was a small desk in Albert's private residence. A cleaning service was hired to clean Father Dunkel's residence and office. A worker approached the desk, lifted the blotter and looked at a sealed envelope. She read, "To be opened when I die." She gave it to Fr. Richards who opened it.

He read,

> I seek forgiveness for many sins. I am truly sorry for causing three students at the University of Notre Dame to be denied the Ph.D. degree in physics. My actions were based on envy, jealousy, and pride. The research exceeded my capabilities and this was threatening to me.
>
> I know I hurt many people, including my friend and colleague, Dr. Gary Nix. I will now contact each person that I knowingly hurt to personally apologize and seek forgiveness.

The note was signed by Father Dunkel and was dated, October 28, two days before his death.